About the Author

David Almond's debut novel *Skellig* is one of the most remarkable children's novels published in recent years. *Kit's Wilderness* is his second novel for children.

I grew up in a big family in a small steep town overlooking the River Tyne. It was a place of ancient coal mines, dark terraced streets, strange shops, new estates and wild heather hills. Our lives were filled with mysterious and unexpected events, and the place and its people have given me many of my stories. I always wanted to be a writer, though I told very few people until I was 'grown up'. I've published lots of fiction for adults, and I've won a number of prizes. I write for adults as well as children. I've been a postman, a brush salesman, an editor and a teacher. I've lived by the North Sea, in inner Manchester, in a Suffolk farmhouse, and I wrote my first stories in a remote and dilapidated Norfolk mansion.

Writing can be difficult, but sometimes it really does feel like a kind of magic. I think that stories are living things – among the most important things in the world.

David Almond

Also by David Almond:

Skellig
Heaven Eyes

Other Titles in Signature:

The Fated Sky
Chance of Safety
Henrietta Branford

Hauntings
Nightcomers
Susan Price

Blackthorn, Whitethorn
Rachel Anderson

A Secret Place
Joan Lingard

Kit's Wilderness

David Almond

Hodder Children's Books

a division of Hodder Headline Limited

Thanks to the Hawthornden Trust for the award of a Hawthornden Fellowship in 1997, and to the Arts Council for a Writer's Award in 1998.

First published in Great Britain in 1999
by Hodder Children's Books

10 9 8

A Catalogue record for this book is available
from the British Library

ISBN 0 340 72716 0

Typeset by Avon Dataset Ltd, Bidford-on-Avon, Warks

Printed and bound in Great Britain by
Clays Ltd, St Ives plc

Hodder Children's Books
A Division of Hodder Headline Limited
338 Euston Road
London NW1 3BH

For Sara Jane

Part One

AUTUMN

They thought we had disappeared, and they were wrong. They thought we were dead, and they were wrong. We stumbled together out of the ancient darkness into the shining valley. The sun glared down on us. The whole world glistened with ice and snow. We held our arms against the light and stared in wonder at each other. We were scorched and blackened from the flames. There was dried blood on our lips, cuts and bruises on our skin. Our eyes began to burn with joy and we laughed, and touched each other and started to walk down together towards Stoneygate. Down there, our neighbours were digging for us in the snow. Policemen were dragging the river bed for us. The children saw us first and started running. Their voices echoed with astonishment and joy: Here they are! Oh, here they are! *They clustered around us. They watched us as if we were ghosts, or creatures from some weird dream.* Here they are! *they whispered.* Look at them. Look at the state of them!

Yes, here we were, the children who had disappeared, brought back into the world as if by magic: John Askew, the blackened boy with bone necklaces and paintings on him; Allie Keenan, the good-bad ice girl with silver skin and claws; the wild dog Jax; and me, Kit

Watson, with ancient stories in my head and ancient pebbles in my palm.

We kept on walking towards our homes with the children whispering and giggling at our side. We smiled and smiled. Who could have known that we would walk together with such happiness, after all we'd been through? At times it seemed that there would be no end to it, that there would just be darkness, that there would be no light. It started with a game, a game we played in the autumn. I played it first on the day the clocks went back.

One

In Stoneygate there was a wilderness. It was an empty space between the houses and the river, where the ancient pit had been. That's where we played Askew's game, the game called Death. We used to gather at the school's gates after the bell had rung. We stood there whispering and giggling. After five minutes, Bobby Carr told us it was time and he led us through the wilderness to Askew's den, a deep hole dug into the earth with old doors slung across it as an entrance and a roof. The place was hidden from the school and from the houses of Stoneygate by the slope and by the tall grasses growing around it. The wild dog Jax waited for us there. When Jax began to growl, Askew drew one of the doors aside. He looked out at us, checked the faces, called us down.

We stumbled one by one down the crumbling steps. We crouched against the walls. The floor was hard-packed clay. Candles burned in niches in the walls. There was a heap of bones in a corner. Askew told us they were human bones, discovered when he'd dug this place. There was a blackened ditch where a fire burned in winter. The den was lined with dried mud. Askew had carved pictures of us all, of animals, of the dogs and cats we owned, of the wild dog, Jax, of imagined monsters and demons, of the gates of Heaven and the snapping jaws of Hell. He wrote into the walls the names of all of us who'd died in there. My friend Allie Keenan sat across the den from me. The blankness in her eyes said: You're on your own down here.

Askew wore black jeans, black trainers, a black T-shirt with 'Megadeth' in white across it. He lit a cigarette and passed it round the ring. He passed around a jug of water that he said was special water, collected from a spring that had its source in the blocked-up tunnels of the ancient coal mine far below. He crouched at the centre, sharpening his sheath knife on a stone. His dark hair tumbled across his eyes, his pale face flickered in the candlelight.

'You have come into this ancient place to play the game called Death,' he whispered.

He laid the knife at the centre on a square of glass. He eyed us all. We chewed our lips, held our breath, our hearts thudded. Sometimes a squeak of fear from someone, sometimes a stifled snigger.

'Whose turn is it to die?' he whispered.

He spun the knife.

We chanted: 'Death Death Death Death . . .'

And then the knife stopped, pointing at the player.

The player had to reach out, to take Askew's hand. Askew drew him from the fringes to the centre.

'There will be a death this day,' said Askew.

The player had to kneel before Askew, then to crouch on all fours. He had to breathe deeply and slowly, then quickly and more quickly still. He had to lift his head and stare into Askew's eyes. Askew held the knife before his face.

'Do you abandon life?' said Askew.

'I abandon life.'

'Do you truly wish to die?'

'I truly wish to die.'

Askew held his shoulder. He whispered gently into his ear, then with his thumb and index finger he closed the player's eyes and said, 'This is Death.'

And the player fell to the floor, dead still, while the rest of us gathered in a ring around him.

'Rest in peace,' said Askew.

'Rest in peace,' said all of us.

Then Askew slid the door aside and we climbed out into the light. Askew came out last. He slid the door back into place, leaving the dead one in the dark.

We lay together in the long grass, in the sunlight, by the shining river.

Askew crouched apart from us, smoking a cigarette, hunched over, sunk in his gloom.

We waited for the dead one to come back.

Sometimes the dead came quickly back to us. Sometimes it took an age, and on those days our whispering and sniggering came to an end. We glanced nervously at each other, chewed our nails. As time went on, the more nervous ones lifted their school bags, glanced fearfully at Askew, set off singly or in pairs towards home. Sometimes we whispered of sliding the door back in order to check on our friend down there, but Askew, without turning to us, would snap,

'No. Death has its own time. Wake him now and all he'll know for ever after is a waking death.'

So we waited, in silence and dread. In the end, everyone came back. We saw at last the white fingers gripping the door from below. The door slid back. The player scrambled out. He blinked in the light, stared at us. He grinned sheepishly, or stared in amazement, as if emerged from an astounding dream.

Askew didn't move.

'Resurrection, eh?' he murmured. He laughed drily to himself.

We gathered around the dead one.

'What was it like?' we whispered. 'What was it like?'

We left Askew hunched there by the river, strolled back together through the wilderness with the dead one in our midst.

Two

I'd only been in Stoneygate a week when Askew found me. I was alone at the edge of the wilderness, standing against the broken fence. I stared out across this new place, the wide space of beaten grass where dozens of children played.

'Kit Watson?'

I turned and found him there. He climbed over and stood beside me. He was broad-faced, broad-shouldered. His hair hung heavy on his brow. A thin moustache was visible on his lip. He held a sketch pad under his arm, had a pencil behind his ear. I'd already seen him in school, lounging bitterly outside a closed classroom door.

'Kit Watson?' he repeated.

I nodded. I caught the scent of dog on him. I shifted away from him. I felt the skin crawling on my neck.

'What is it?' I said. My throat felt dry, my tongue felt too big for my mouth.

He smiled, and pointed to our house, across the potholed lane behind us, behind its own fence and its narrow garden.

'Just moved in, eh?'

'My Dad came from here. And my grandfather.'

I tried to say it proudly, to let him know I had the right to be here in Stoneygate.

'I know that, Kit.' He held out a packet of sweets. 'Go on. Take one.'

I chewed the sweet.

'You're from the old families. That's good, Kit. You're one of us.' He contemplated me. 'Been watching you, Kit, ever since you come.'

He waved his arm, indicating the kids at their games: football, fighting, little kids skipping or playing shops and houses. 'There's something to you,' he said. 'Something different to this rabble.' He stared, like he was waiting for me to reply.

'What d'you mean?'

'What do I mean? That you're like me, Kit.'

I looked at him, the thick body, the darkness in his eyes. '*No*,' I thought. '*No. I'm not like you.*'

He pointed out again. 'What do you see out there?'

'Eh?'

'Eh? Eh? Out there. What d'you see?'

I looked across the wilderness. 'Kids. Grass. River. Same as you see.'

He grinned. 'Aye. That's right. That's all, eh?'

I looked again. 'Yes.'

He laughed and shook his head. He slid a sheet of paper from his sketch pad. 'Made this for you,' he said. 'Go on.'

It was me, a charcoal drawing. Me sitting against the chain

link fence at school, as I had two days ago, staring down into the grass.

'Good, eh?' he said. 'Just like you, eh?'

I nodded.

'Best artist in the school. Not that it counts for nothing in that blasted place.'

I held it towards him. He laughed. 'Go on,' he said. 'It's yours. Take it home and pin it on your wall. An Askew original. Collector's item.'

I rolled it carefully, held it in my fist.

'Not very happy that day, were you?'

I shrugged

'No mates yet, eh?' he said.

I blinked, shrugged again. 'Yeah.'

'Not proper, though, eh? Not yet, eh?' He kept casting his eyes across me, staring at me, assessing me. 'You'll come to see more.'

'What d'you mean?'

'You'll come to see there's more,' he said. 'You'll come to see the others that walk beside us in the world.'

'What others?'

He shook his head. 'Nowt. Don't let it bother you for now. But we'll get closer, Kit. Me and you. We'll get so close it'll be like we're joined in blood.'

I looked away from the darkness in his eyes. I shifted backwards from the scent of him. I wanted him gone, wanted to be left alone again.

He nodded, started to move away. 'There's a bunch of us,'

he said. He looked into the wilderness. 'Him,' he said.

I followed his eyes.

'And her, and him, and him, and her. Others. Good mates. Special. Kids that's different to the rabble.'

I followed with my eyes, saw the children he pointed to, those I would come to know, those who would step down with me into Askew's den. There was Daniel Sharkey, Louise McCall, Wilfie Cook, Dot Gullane. Ordinary children, nothing to mark them out except the fact that they came from the old families of Stoneygate, and that they were the ones to play the game called Death.

He held out the sweets to me again. 'You as well,' he said. 'You most of all. You're like me, Kit. You think you're different, but you'll come to see that me and you is just the same.' He winked, patted my shoulder. 'Askew,' he said. 'John Askew.' He watched me for a while. 'It's like I've been waiting for you,' he said. 'Expecting you.'

Then he grinned, turned, strolled away. Two girls stood up as he approached, walked away from him. The little blond boy I already knew as Bobby Carr ran towards him. The wild dog Jax was running at Bobby's heels.

'Askew!' Bobby yelled. 'John Askew!'

Askew waited till Bobby and Jax were at his side, then they wandered on.

My mother came out from the house to my side. 'Made a friend?' she said.

I shrugged.

'Looks kind of rough,' she said.

'Dunno,' I said. 'John Askew, he's called.'

'Oh,' she said. 'One of that lot . . . But we mustn't be guided only by appearances, or by the family that produced him.'

I showed her the drawing. She whistled.

'Now there's a talent,' she said. 'Must be something to him, eh?'

We looked again. Askew, Bobby and the dog went over the edge towards the river. I watched, saw nothing else. Just the kids, the wilderness, the river. I felt my hands trembling, felt the sweat on my palms. That night I dreamed I followed him through the night across the wilderness. I woke up dreaming that his hands were at my throat.

Three

Soon afterwards he came to me again. It was in school this time. I was in the corridor below the art room. Some of his drawings were displayed there. They were dark things, black things: silhouettes of children on a grey field; black slow river; black tilting houses; black scratches of birds in a sullen sky. He imagined the old life in the pit below, and he drew the hunched bodies of boys and men in the tunnels, the squat pit ponies, all black on black except for tiny chinks of white given by candles or hooded lamps.

'Good, eh?' he said.

I nodded. 'Brilliant.'

He showed me how the children in his pictures stooped and grimaced, how their bodies were twisted and stunted by the demands of the pit.

'Poor sods,' he said. 'Our ancestors was like that, Kit. Stunted life, pain then death. You ever think that?'

'Yeah.'

'Ha. I'll bet. Don't know we're born these days, Kit. A hundred years ago that'd've been us down there, John Askew and Kit Watson, crawling on their bellies in the darkness down below. Where the walls collapse and the gas explodes and there's bodies lying in the blocked-off shafts.'

A teacher walked by, Miss Bush. 'Good morning, Christopher,' she said.

'Good morning, Miss.'

She stared at me. 'Hurry to your lesson now.'

'Yes, Miss.'

'You as well, John Askew.'

Askew glowered. His face flushed. 'Burning Bush,' he muttered as she walked away. 'Don't take no notice of that old cow.'

I moved away from him.

'Seen your story,' he said.

'Eh?'

'Your story. The one they put up on the wall.'

'Oh.'

It was an old tale, one my grandfather had told me.

'Good one,' he said. 'Brilliant.'

'Thanks.'

He held my arm as I tried to move away.

'Your stories is like my drawings, Kit. They take you back deep into the dark and show it lives within us still.' He lifted my face, made me stare into his eyes. 'You understand?' he said.

I tried to look away. My hands trembled and my flesh crawled, but I felt myself being drawn to him.

'You do,' he said. 'You see it, don't you? You're starting to see that you and me is just the same. It's like we've been together for a long long time.' He smiled as I pulled away. 'You seen the monument?' he said.

'Eh?'

'Eh? Eh? The monument, Kit. Get your Grandpa to take you. Then you'll start to see more.'

'We're getting together after school,' he said as I turned away. 'Bobby Carr, a few more. You'll see them outside the gates. If you're interested.'

I shrugged.

'It's just a game,' he said. 'A bit of fun. Outside the gates, if you're interested.' He pressed a finger to his lips. 'Keep it quiet but. Tell none of them in here.'

I didn't go that time, but in the end it was as if I couldn't help myself.

Four

We came to Stoneygate because Grandma died and Grandpa was left alone. We bought the house at Stoneygate's edge, one of a long line that faced the wilderness and the river. Grandpa moved into the room next to mine. He had a single trunk of clothes and souvenirs. He put his old pit helmet and his polished pitman's lamp on the shelf above his bed. He hung a photograph of himself and Grandma on the wall. The photograph was fading and there were hundreds of tiny cracks on its surface. It showed them on their wedding day at St. Thomas' Church. He wore a smart black suit and a white flower in his buttonhole. Grandma held a massive white bouquet before her long white dress. They smiled and smiled. Just beyond them you could see the graves, then Stoneygate, then the hills and the distant misty moors.

At first Grandpa was gloomy, watery-eyed and silent. He hardly seemed to know me. I heard Mum whispering that Grandma's death would mean the death of him as well. At night he used to sigh and whisper in his room as I dropped off to sleep next door. I dreamed that Grandma was with him again, just beyond the thin wall beside my bed, that she had come to comfort him as he died. I heard her voice, soothing him. I dreamed that his sighs were his final breaths. I trembled with fear that I would be the one to hear him die.

But he didn't die. He started to smile again, and tell his tales and sing his ancient pit songs in his hoarse cracked voice:

When I was young and in me prime,
Eh, aye, I could hew . . .

He took me walking and showed me that the evidence of the pit was everywhere – depressions in the gardens, jagged cracks in the roadways and in the house walls. Lamp posts and telegraph poles were twisted and skewed. Fragments of coal darkened the soil. He told me how things had been in his day: the huge black slag heap beside the river, the great wheels and winding gear, the hundreds of men disappearing every morning and every night into the earth. He showed me where the entrances to the shafts had been, told me about the dizzying drop in the cage to the tunnels far below. He pointed up to the hills past Stoneygate, told me they were filled with shafts, potholes, ancient drift mines.

'Look at the earth and you think it's solid,' he said. 'But look deeper and you'll see it's riddled with tunnels. A warren. A labyrinth.'

As we wandered, I used to keep on asking him: How deep did you go? How dark was it? What was it like to go down there, day after day, week after week, year after year? Why weren't you terrified, Grandpa?

He used to smile.

'It was very deep, Kit. Very dark. And every one of us was scared of it. As a lad I'd wake up trembling, knowing that as a Watson born in Stoneygate I'd soon be following my ancestors into the pit.'

He used to draw me close to him, touch my cheek, run his fingers through my hair.

'But there was more than just the fear, Kit. We were also driven to it. We understood our fate. There was the strangest joy in dropping down together into the darkness that we feared. And most of all there was the joy of coming out again together into the lovely world. Bright spring mornings, brilliant sunshine, birdsong, walking together through the lovely hawthorn lanes towards our homes.'

Grandpa used to swing his arms and sing out loud and turn his face towards the sun. He used to grip my shoulders and smile and smile and I felt his body trembling with the love he held for me.

'This is our world,' he used to say. 'Aye, there's more than enough of darkness in it. But over everything there's all this joy, Kit. There's all this lovely lovely light.'

One Saturday morning I woke early and heard him singing. I went to his room.

'Grandpa,' I said. 'What's the monument?'

He laughed.

'Aye,' he said. 'That's another thing on my list to show you.'

And we crept out of the silent house and he took me to

St. Thomas' graveyard. A pretty place: old stone church, old trees, leaning headstones.

'Through here,' he said.

We followed the narrow pathway between the graves. We came to a larger grave, a high narrow pyramid. It was a monument to the Stoneygate pit disaster. It happened in 1821. A hundred and seventeen were killed. The stone was worn by rain and wind and age, but the long list of names remained. Nine year olds, ten year olds, eleven year olds, twelve year olds. The sun poured down through the ancient trees on us, dappling the stone, the earth and us with the shadows of trembling leaves.

'Imagine it, eh?' he said.

I reached up and ran my finger across the names. I caught my breath. Right at the top was the name I knew.

'*John Askew*,' I said. '*Aged thirteen.*'

'Aye. There's lots of names you know on this old list, son.' He smiled. 'You ready?'

'Eh?'

'Watch.'

He took my hand, gently drew my finger to the foot of the stone. The names there were becoming unreadable, worn away by trickling water and rising damp. Bright green moss grew over the letters.

He scraped away the moss with his fingernails. I read the final name, caught my breath again, felt the thudding of my heart.

'Aye, Kit.'

He smiled. 'A great great great great uncle? Yours was always one of the family names.'

I traced it with my finger: *Christopher Watson, aged thirteen.*

He put his arm around me. 'Don't let it trouble you, Kit. It's long ago.'

I picked more moss away from the base of the stone.

Neither can they die any more, for they are equal unto the angels.

Grandpa smiled.

'All it shows is how you're in your rightful place now: back at home in Stoneygate.'

He looked into my eyes.

'OK?' he whispered.

I gazed back into his dark and tender eyes. 'OK,' I said.

I stared at our two names. John Askew, Christopher Watson, with the long list of the dead between us, joining us. I kept turning as Grandpa led me away, until the mark of my name had blended once again with moss and stone.

'Used to get a laugh here long ago,' he said. 'Used to come at night as kids. Used to dance in a ring around the monument and chant the *Our Father* backwards. Used to say we'd see the faces of those old pit kids blooming in the dark.' He giggled. 'Bloody terrifying. Used to belt home laughing and screaming, scared half to death. Kids' games, eh? What they like?'

He put his arm around me as we walked home.

'It's great that you've come here,' he said. 'I've wanted this, wanted to show you where you've come from, where we've all come from.' He patted my shoulder. 'Don't let it trouble you. The world's so different now.'

He pointed out across the wilderness.

'We used to say we saw the ancient pit kids playing down there by the river. They'd come out from the dark. The ones they hadn't been able to get out from the blocked tunnels. The ones that hadn't been properly buried.'

'And did you?'

'We said we did. Sometimes I almost believed we did. I squinted, saw them there at dusk, on misty days, days when the sun glared and the earth shimmered, days when the things you see seem to shift and change . . .' He laughed. 'Who knows, Kit? We were young. You start to believe anything when you're young. And it was all so long ago.'

That night, I stared out from my window across the wilderness, watched for skinny children playing. I narrowed my eyes, squinted, saw nothing but a dark thick-set form walking above the river, a black dog at its heels. John Askew, aged thirteen, watched by Christopher Watson, aged thirteen.

Five

It was Grandpa who showed me Askew's place. We wandered one day towards the fringes of Stoneygate, where the houses petered out and the hills started. Skylarks flew up from the turf before us, gulls flew in with the mist from the sea. There were lanes that followed the tracks of abandoned coal lines, fields and paddocks that rose towards distant dark and misty moors. Ruined stone walls, ruined cottages with weeds growing through gaping windows. All around were ancient hawthorn hedges, red berries burning brightly among the dark green tiny leaves.

'Went nesting here as a lad,' Grandpa said. 'Shinned up to the nests, popped the egg into my mouth, clambered down to my mates. Cut pinholes in them, blew the insides out, rested them in neat rows in boxes of sand. Not a thing that's done these days. Against the law. But then it was what all lads did. And there were rules: don't leave any less than two, don't destroy the nest. Rules that let the bird families survive, generation after generation.'

Grandpa cast his eyes across the steepening landscape,

pointed to where the disappeared pits once were.

'Now it's proper countryside again,' he said. 'A great place for you to live and grow. Great place for young life to flourish.'

And he closed his eyes and smiled and listened to the larks, dark tiny specks that belted out their songs from high up in the sky.

The Askews lived in the final street, a potholed cul-de-sac of old pit cottages before the hills started. Most of the cottages were boarded up. Close by were a shuttered Co-op Store and a tumbledown pub, The Fox.

Grandpa pointed into the cul-de-sac. A skinny dog roamed there, its tail curled up between its legs.

'That's the one,' he said. 'In the corner there. Where your mate lives.'

Curtains were closed at the windows. There was an upturned pram in the beaten garden, an empty rabbit hutch. We stood for a moment. We saw the curtains tugged aside a few inches, a woman's face peeping out. Nothing but the dog moved. There was sudden music from another of the houses, a heavy pounding beat, then a woman's bitter scream, and silence again. The woman at Askew's window stared. She stood in front of the curtain, holding a baby in her arms, watching us.

'The mother,' said Grandpa, and we turned away.

We met the father as we passed The Fox. He stumbled out, cupped a cigarette to his mouth and tried to light it. He muttered and cursed, leaned against the pub wall, flashed his eyes at us. His face was red and strained.

Grandpa nodded at him. 'Askew,' he said in greeting.

The man stared at us, blinked, refocused. 'It's you,' he said. 'Watson.'

'Aye,' said Grandpa. 'And this is my lad. My son's lad, Christopher.'

He glared at me, spat down on to the broken pavement.

'Christopher Watson, eh?' he said. He wiped his lips with his sleeve. He coughed and cursed. 'So what am I to do, eh? Kiss his bloody precious feet, eh?' He stuck his head forward. 'Eh?' he said. 'Eh?' Then laughed and coughed and cursed again.

Grandpa drew me on, back towards home, back towards the wilderness, where we passed through the children playing and came upon Askew himself. Jax was at his side. He sat on a rock above the river with his sketch pad on his knees. His hand moved quickly across the paper. He turned and saw us there, and his face darkened. I raised my hand, but he ignored me and quickly turned towards his work again. The dog Jax watched us and growled.

'A guided tour of the Askews,' said Grandpa as we walked back home. He laughed. 'They're like the Watsons. True Stoneygate folk. Generation after generation of them, stretching back into the deep dark past. And aye, they've always been a queer crew, but when you needed a mate, they was always there.'

Later that evening, he knocked on my door. 'Thought I had this somewhere,' he said. He showed me a little pit pony carved from coal. 'Lovely, eh?' he said.

I held it in my palm. It was black and smooth as glass, worn by time, but you saw how real it was, how sharp its detail had been.

'Carved by that lad's Grandpa,' he said. 'Many years ago.'

'Askew's an artist as well,' I said.

I showed him the drawing that Askew had done of me.

'That's how it goes,' he said. 'Things passing down generation to generation.'

Six

It was Allie Keenan who helped to draw me in. I walked through the gates one afternoon and saw Askew's group gathering there. There was Bobby Carr, the others, then Allie standing silent on the fringes. She saw me watching and she grinned. She was in my year. She lived behind us in one of the houses by the green at Stoneygate's heart. One morning she'd run to catch up with me as I walked to school.

'Name's Allie Keenan,' she said. 'Knew your Grandma. Used to babysit me sometimes when I was little. Led her a dance but she loved it really.' She laughed. 'She used to tell me about her precious little Kit. Perfectly behaved, she used to say. Not like one little madam I could mention.'

We walked on together.

'Perfectly behaved,' she said. 'Is that still true? Was it ever true?' She watched me and grinned.

'Dunno,' I said.

'Certainly the proper gent in class,' she said. 'Or is that just the new boy's way?' She kept on watching me, kept on grinning.

'Dunno,' I said. 'Dunno what to say.'

'Ha. Butter wouldn't melt, eh?'

We kept on walking.

'She was so lovely, though,' she said. 'Must have been awful for you. We were all so sad when she passed away.'

Allie was little and thin and got into trouble for the lipstick and eye shadow she wore in school. She wore red shoes and yellow jeans. In class she giggled at the teachers and hunched over her books and scribbled fast and frantic stories filled with dragons and monsters and maidens in distress. In lessons she hated, like Geography, she stared out of the window and picked her nails and daydreamed about being in a soap on television one day.

'So?' asked Mr Dobbs, the Geography teacher one day. 'So, Miss Alison Keenan, what have you learned of terminal moraines in the last half hour?'

Allie blinked, refocused, pondered.

'Forgive me, Mr Dobbs,' she said. 'But I simply fail to see the relevance of the subject to a person of my inclinations and ambitions.'

For that she was given detention and a warning letter was sent home.

The morning after I saw her at the school gates we walked together again to school.

'You're one of John Askew's friends,' I said.

She looked at me, her lips tight shut. 'Hm,' she said.

'I saw you with the others, at the gates.'

'Hm,' she said again. She quickened her step.

'OK. You're not, then,' I said.

I let her get ahead of me, but she hesitated. 'Why d'you want to know?' she said. She turned and stared right at me.

'Dunno,' I said. 'There's something . . .'

'Something! He's just a brute. He's a cave man.'

'I talked to him.'

'And he grunted back, I bet.' She just watched me, hands on hips.

I chewed my lips. I wanted to tell her that I saw how brutal Askew might be, but that I felt drawn to him. I wanted to tell her that I'd begun to believe what he said was true: that I was like him, that he was like me. I thought of what my Grandpa said about the pit, that he was terrified of it, but that he was driven to it. But as she stood there with her eyebrows raised and her head tilted to the side, I knew she'd just laugh and scoff.

'Listen,' she said. 'From what I've seen of you I don't really think we're the thing for you.'

I looked away.

'Mr New Boy,' she said. 'Mr Perfectly Behaved.' She tapped her foot and pondered. 'He's a cave man,' she said again. 'You know that, don't you? If you don't know how to deal with him, he'll cause you all kinds of bother. You stick to your homework and your stories, Mr New Boy.'

I shrugged.

'He'd have you for breakfast,' she said. She pondered again, then shook her head. 'Look at you,' she said. 'Somebody's got to protect you, haven't they?'

Then she turned and danced away.

Seven

I woke with a start in the middle of the night.

'There he is! After him, lads! there he is!'

It was Grandpa, calling out.

Then silence. *Just one of his dreams,* I thought. I smiled, turned over and began to sleep again.

'Aye! Aye! Again! Follow him, lads!'

The wall beside me trembled. I heard how he twisted and turned in his bed.

I pulled a shirt and shorts on, tiptoed out, tiptoed to him, sat on his bedside. His legs kicked and his arms jerked. He was panting, gasping for breath.

'Grandpa,' I whispered. 'Grandpa.' I spread my hand over his brow. 'Grandpa.'

His eyes opened, stared, reflected the light from the moon that shone in through his window.

'Aye, that's him!' he said. 'After him! After him!'

I held his shoulder, shook him gently. 'Grandpa. Grandpa.'

He blinked, shook his head. 'Eh? What's that?'

'It's me, Grandpa. Kit.'

I leaned across and switched the bedside lamp on.

He stared again, seeing me now. He let out his breath in a long sigh.

'Kit. It's you, Kit.' He shook his head again, squeezed his eyes and smiled. 'Ach. And we almost had him that time.'

He laughed and eased himself up, leaned back against the headboard. He glanced at the clock and grinned.

'Old blokes and lads should be asleep at this time of the night, eh?' He pressed a finger to his lips. 'They'll have our guts for garters, Kit.'

'Who was it?' I whispered.

'Little Silky.'

'Silky?'

'Called him that cos of the way the lamplight fell on him. Cos it made him shine like flickering silk as he flashed through the tunnels before our eyes. A glimpse, and then he's gone.'

'A ghost?'

'Little lad in shorts and boots that many of us seen down there. Sometimes just looking at us from the deepest edges of the dark, sometimes slipping past our backs as we leaned down to the coal.' He smiled. 'If ever a lamp went out or a pitman's bait was pinched, that's Silky's work, we'd say. Little mischief, little Silky. A glimpse, and then he's gone.'

He smiled again. His eyes looked deep into the past, deep into the pit.

'Some said he'd been trapped down there after one of the disasters. One they'd never been able to get to. One of those that never got taken out and buried. Not scary, though. Something sweet in him. Something you wanted to touch and comfort and draw into the light.' He smiled. 'Ask any of the old blokes left round here and they'll tell you about our Silky.'

He stroked his chin.

'Sometimes chased him, like in the dream, but never got to touch him.'

Someone stirred in another part of the house.

Grandpa switched the light off. 'Guts for garters, Kit,' he whispered. 'Back to bed, eh?'

We looked at each other, faces blooming in the moonlight.

'Used to leave out biscuits for him, cups of water,' he whispered.

'And he took them?'

'It seemed he took them.' He smiled again. 'A thing of brightness,' he whispered, 'deep down there in the dark.' He squeezed my arm. 'Often wonder if he's down there still,' he whispered. 'Night, son.'

'Goodnight.'

I tiptoed back to bed, back to sleep.

I lay a long time with the moonlight flooding in on me. I saw him from the corner of my eye. He shimmered in the moonlight in the corner of my room.

'Silky!' I whispered.

I tried to focus on him but he just kept shifting to the edges of my vision. I reached out to him but he faded into the dark.

'Silky,' I whispered as I fell asleep.

'Silky!' I called as I entered my dreams. He was there, flickering in front of me. He started to run, and I followed him. Sometimes he stopped and turned and watched me and I saw his shorts, his boots, his skinny body, his gentle face. All that night I followed him.

'Silky!' I kept calling. 'Silky! Silky!'

He ran all night before me, flickering through the endless tunnels of my dreams.

Eight

It was late afternoon, the day the clocks went back. I was wandering alone. I found them gathered by the school gates. Allie, Bobby, a little crowd of others. Beyond them, the dark figure of Askew lurched towards the river with Jax at his side. I paused, my heart thudded, my palms were soaked. Allie saw me standing there. She pursed her lips and turned away. I went towards them, stood at the fringes. They watched me, suspicious.

'Who asked you?' hissed Wilfie Cook.

Bobby grinned. 'S'all right,' he said, in his high soft voice.

Askew disappeared. We waited.

'OK,' said Bobby, and the group moved out across the wilderness.

I trailed behind. I kept slowing, hesitating, kept telling myself to stop, to go home. Allie strode at the front of the group and didn't look back. The slope steepened. We waded through the long grass above the river and came to the den. When we were all gathered there, dead still and dead silent, Jax barked and Askew's hand appeared and drew the door aside. He looked up into our faces. His eyes met mine and he grinned.

'Come inside,' he said.

I was the last to go down. I crouched like the others against the wall. Askew slid the door shut. He lit the cigarette, he poured the water.

'There's a new one come to play our game,' he said.

All of them but Allie stared at me. I saw the excitement in their eyes, heard the sniggers. The cup of water in my hand trembled.

'He's chicken,' whispered Louise.

There were giggles, then Askew whispered, 'Silence!' He looked around the den. 'What should we do with him?' he asked.

'Skin him,' hissed Bobby.

'Needles down his fingernails,' said Louise.

'The Voodoo Slits,' whispered Dot.

Allie looked down, down.

Askew snorted.

'What must we really do?' he said.

They breathed in and waited for his voice to lead them, then they spoke together.

'We must welcome him,' they said.

'What must he keep?' said Askew.

'The secret,' they answered.

'What must he give to us?'

'Life.'

'What do we promise him?'

'Death.'

He leaned towards me, his heavy body loomed in the candlelight.

'Do you agree,' he said, 'to keep the secrets of this gathering, to tell no one of our game?'

I glanced at Allie. She made a face, poked her tongue out at me, looked away.

'Yes,' I said.

'Drink the water,' Askew whispered.

I took the jug from him with trembling hands and drank from it.

'Smoke the cigarette.'

I took the cigarette and drew on it.

He smiled. 'And now the knife.' He held it before my eyes. 'Kiss the knife.'

I kissed the cold steel. He pressed the point against my lips.

'Understand,' he whispered. 'If you break our trust, the mad dog Jax will tear you limb from limb.'

'Limb from limb,' the others whispered.

'This is Kit,' said Askew. 'The new one. Any damage done to him is damage done to all of us. Will we avenge him?'

'We will avenge him,' they whispered.

He smiled deep into my eyes.

'One day, Kit Watson,' he whispered, 'you will see your name written on these walls. You will join the long list of the dead.'

He touched my cheek.

'Your name will be written here, just as it's written on the tombstone.'

I stared past him to the names. At the head of the list was written, *John Askew, aged thirteen.* Many of those beneath were already worn away by trickling water, then there was an empty space beneath.

'Now,' he said. 'Let us play the game called Death.'

He laid the knife on the glass and set it spinning.

It didn't point at me that day.

Nine

Saturday morning she came knocking at the door.

'Somebody for you, Kit!' Mum called. 'A friend of yours. Alison.'

I went down and found them talking and laughing about Grandma on the step.

Allie led me out of the garden, across the fence and into the wilderness.

'You're a stupid fool,' she said.

'Eh?'

'A stupid fool. Only here a few weeks and already you're in with that daft lot.'

'You're in with them.'

She threw her hands into the air.

'Jeez,' she said. 'I can see you're going to drive me wild! Have you seen them? Have you really looked at them and seen them? Bunch of wimps and jerks and thickos and no-hopers. And that brute at the middle of them, hunking and lurching like a cave man. It's a farce, man.'

'What about you, then?'

'Oh, you perfect behaviour stupid nincompoop!' She stamped the ground and glared at me. 'It's called experience. It's called getting to know what goes on in the stupid world. It's called watching other people's stupid behaviour and getting to know how people work.'

She strode away. She shook her head and swung her arms. She kicked out at a massive thistle. She turned round and pointed at herself.

'I'm going to be an actor,' she said. 'An artist. I need to see these things cos the day'll come when I'll be able to act the thickos out!' She glared at me again.

'And you . . .' she said.

'Me what?'

'Exactly! You what? Mr Nice. Mr Perfect. Mr Butter Wouldn't Melt. What's your plans, eh? Join the Civil Service or run a computer shop or God help us – yes, that's it! – a teacher! Yes sir, Mr Watson. No sir, Mr Watson. Can I go to the toilet, Mr Watson, sir?'

She burst out laughing and kicked the thistle again and the seedhead exploded into the air. 'Is that right?' she said. She looked at me. She giggled. 'It is! It is!'

And she ran away laughing towards the river and flung herself down into the grass.

By the time I reached her she sat up chewing a stem of grass. She pursed her lips and didn't look at me as I sat a few feet away from her. I watched the river flowing, saw how it churned at the centre as the tide turned.

'Have you died?' I whispered.

She clicked her tongue, said nothing.

'Died!' she said at last.

'Have you?'

'Once.'

'What was it like?'

'Hell's teeth, Kit.' She shuffled angrily, as if she wanted to run again. 'You will,' she said. 'You'll drive me wild.' She bit the grass, spat the end of the stem out. 'Yes,' she said. 'I died. But I pretended.' She giggled. 'Made them wait, though. Hardly anybody left when I came back out.'

'What did you tell them?'

'All the usual stuff. Bright lights at the end of tunnels. Dark rivers. Devils and demons. Angels singing. All that stuff.' She giggled again. 'Good bit of acting, that.' She turned and looked at me and shook her head. 'They all do,' she said. 'Everybody.'

'Pretend?'

'Yes. Pretend. They say they don't, but they do.'

'How do you know?'

'Just do. Thickos and louts, that's what they do.'

I thought about the dark den, what it would be like to be alone down there, what it might be like to be dead.

'But you couldn't know,' I said. 'Could you? There's no way of knowing if they pretend or if it's real.'

She glared at me.

'No, sir, Mr Watson. Of course you're perfectly right, sir, Mr Watson.'

'You think you know everything,' I said. 'You think everything's just a game. You think everything's for your own stupid entertainment.' I felt tears running from my eyes. 'People *do* die. People *do*. People *do*.'

I lay staring down into the grass. I heard Grandpa's songs running through my head. I heard Grandma's far-off whispering.

'They do,' I softly said again, and the words were carried away across the wilderness on the breeze.

Allie shuffled closer.

'Jeez,' she whispered. 'I was right. You do need somebody to protect you.' I felt her watching me.

'Trouble with you is,' she said. 'You're not one of the louts or thickos or a no-hopers. And you're not in it for fun like me. Left to yourself you'd be begging Askew to dig a hole and chuck you in.' She tapped my skull. 'Hey,' she whispered. 'Hey. Mister Watson. Mister Innocent.'

'What?' I muttered.

'I'm just looking after you,' she said. 'Like your Grandma would have wanted me to.'

'How d'you know what she wanted?'

She sighed and clicked her tongue.

'Tell you what,' she said. 'I'll stop going to the game as well, eh? I'm sick of it anyway, being down there with that lot and that lout. We'll start doing other things together, eh?'

I stood up and squeezed the tears from my eyes.

'You haven't got a clue, have you?' I said. 'What if I *want* to play? What if I *want* to see what really happens?'

And I hurried away from her across the wilderness, past the kids playing, squeezing back my tears.

Ten

'Look at this,' said Grandpa.

I was in my room, doing homework, something boring about time differences between England and the rest of the world. It was a chilly evening and rain was pouring down on to the wilderness. I kept looking up from my desk, staring out. I worked out that if you travelled fast enough you could get to where you wanted before you even started. I didn't write that, but wrote what they wanted: that if it was such and such a time in Stoneygate, then it would be such and such a time in New York. Boring. Then Grandpa knocked on my door.

He put it on the desk in front of me. It was a flat rectangle of coal, polished like the pony. There were deep imprints on its surface. I ran my fingers across them.

'It's tree bark,' I said.

'That's right. Tree bark. Lots of coal's got tree bark patterns on it if you slice it careful enough.'

'That's what coal was,' I said. 'Trees. Millions of years back.'

'Correct.' He nodded at the window. 'That's what you'd've seen if you sat here then. Massive trees. Swamps. All those millions of years back.' He ran his fingers over the coal. 'There's this as well.' He put a black fossil on the desk. A spiralling horn-shaped shell. 'Guess,' he said.

'Some kind of animal. Something that lived at the same time as the trees.'

'Correct. An ammonite. This is the fossil of its shell. The creature lived inside, like a snail does, or a hermit crab. This too came out of the pit, just like the tree bark.'

I held it in my palm.

'Thing is,' he said. 'It's a creature that lived in the sea.'

I imagined it squirming its way across sand, beneath the water.

'The sea came in and flooded the place and the trees fell down and time passed and the sea laid down sediment that turned to rock and the earth churned and laid down more rock and time passed and the rock thickened and pressed down on the ancient trees and animals and time passed and passed and turned them all to coal.' He laughed. 'But you know this, eh? They've told you this at school?'

I nodded. He laughed again.

'When we dropped down in the cage we dropped through time. Million years a minute. Pitmen. Time travellers.' He ran his hand across my book. 'Very neat. And all the right answers, I'm sure. You'll go a long way, lad.'

I stared out, saw the trees, the swamps, the sea flooding in. Then blinked, and saw the wilderness, the falling rain.

‘Mysterious business,’ he said. ‘It was the light and heat of the sun that made those trees grow. Then they lay pitch black in the pitch black earth. And we come along and dig it out. And what did we want from it? For the heat it gave, for the light it gave.’ He touched the tree bark. ‘This stuff, blacker than the blackest night holding the heat and light of the ancient sun in it.’

He giggled, moved the fossil across the desk as if it was still alive. He slid it onto my written page. ‘It’s for you,’ he said. ‘And the fossil tree as well.’ He slid that on to my page, rested it on my answers, ‘Gifts from a time traveller,’ he said. He touched my shoulder, laughed gently. ‘Giving out my tales and treasures,’ he said. ‘Soon there’ll be nothing left to give.’

I slipped the ammonite into my pocket, told myself I’d keep it with me always now. A treasure from my grandfather. A gift from the deep, dark past.

Eleven

'Look,' said Mum.

It was Saturday afternoon. Bright sunlight. She was at the open window, a gentle cool breeze was coming through.

'Come and look,' she said.

I stood beside her.

'What?' I said.

She put her arm around my shoulder. 'There.'

Askew's father was further along the lane, tottering alongside the fence. He kept stopping. He reeled, held on to the fence, lowered his head, drew deeply on a cigarette.

'Here!' he yelled. 'Get yourself here!'

'Drunk as a lord,' said Mum.

He rocked backwards, caught the fence again. 'Get yourself here!'

'Jack Askew,' she said. 'Drunk as a lord again.'

Then there was Askew himself, head hanging, walking slowly from the river towards the man. His dad called him on, with drunken swings of his arm. And Jax was there, walking slowly too. Shuffling.

'Move it!

Askew reached the fence. The man grabbed his son by the throat, pulled him close. We saw his bare teeth, saliva dripping, his great flushed face. He snarled into the boy's ear. Askew looked down, hung his arms by his side, tried to turn his face away but the man kept dragging it, slapping it back. He whispered, gripped the boy's throat tighter, laughed and snarled. Then he let go, reeled backwards, caught the fence, stood upright, spat, smoked, staggered on along the lane.

'And let that be a lesson to you!' he yelled. He turned to the houses. 'What you looking at?' he shouted. 'Eh? What you looking at?'

We took a step backward away from the window. He went on glaring, reeling. Cigarette smoke streamed from his open lips.

'Imagine,' said Mum. 'Imagine having to live with that, having to put up with that.'

I nodded, and felt her hand stroking my shoulder.

'You'd have to get so tough,' she said.

'Or pretend to be tough.'

'Yes, or pretend to be tough.'

Jack Askew staggered onwards. His son watched him for a moment, then he eased himself to the ground, and leaned back against the fence. He sat there with his head hung low and his arm around Jax. We saw his shoulders trembling.

'Poor lad,' whispered Mum. 'Poor soul.'

Twelve

Askew's den. The floor was damp with yesterday's rain. Water had trickled down the walls through Askew's carvings. The scent of damp, of the candles, of the bodies crouching there. Allie faced me through the flickering light. She watched me, but there was nothing in her eyes. I stared at the others, these children like me from the ancient families of Stoneygate. Had something like death really happened to them? Had they really gone through something like the children on the monument? Or was it just a game and they had all pretended? I read their names.

John Askew, aged thirteen; Robert Carr, aged eleven; Wilfred Cook, aged fifteen; Dorothy Gullane, aged twelve; Alison Keenan, aged thirteen; Daniel Sharkey, aged fourteen; Louise McCall, aged thirteen . . .

Below them was the wide space for the names to come, and I saw my own name there, as if I were dreaming.

Christopher Watson, aged thirteen.

All around us were paintings of demons and monsters, of bright beings with great white wings, of the gates of Heaven and the snapping jaws of Hell. The water came to me and I sipped it. The cigarette came to me and I drew on it. I looked at Allie again. She was steely, blank, just returning my gaze. I saw it in her eyes: You're on your own down here, Mr Watson. I wanted to shout across to her, to tell her that she was right, that we should get away from the bunch of louts and no-hopers and find other things to do, but I just sat there and sat there, and the more I sat the more I trembled, the more I was terrified that the knife would point at me that day. But I also wanted it. I was driven to it like Grandpa had been driven to the darkness of the pit. I wanted to know something of what the children on the monument had known, something of what my Grandma had known. I stared down at the knife as Askew laid it on the glass.

'Whose turn is it to die?' he whispered.

'Death,' we chanted. 'Death death death death . . .'

The knife shimmered, spinning. It spun on and on.

Me, I thought, as it spun to me and then away again. Me, not me, me, not me, me, not me . . .

And then it slowed and came to rest.

Me.

I caught my breath, my trembling quickened. I looked across at Allie. On your own, her eyes said. You're on your own.

Askew smiled. He reached out to me. I took his hand. He drew me to the centre. He laid his hand across my head for a moment. I felt the tears in my eyes.

'Calm down, Kit,' he whispered in my ear, but I couldn't

stop the trembling. 'Calm down, Kit Watson.'

I heard Louise: 'He's chicken. He's a chicken.'

I heard the giggles of the others.

'Silence,' whispered Askew. 'There will be a death this day,'

I knelt as I had seen others kneel. I crouched on all fours.

This is nothing, I told myself. *It's just a game, nothing but a game.*

'Breathe deeply and slowly, Kit,' he whispered.

I breathed deeply and slowly.

'Breathe quickly and more quickly.'

I breathed quickly and more quickly.

'Look into my eyes.'

I looked into his eyes. It was like looking into a tunnel of endless dark. I felt myself staring deeper, deeper. I felt myself driven to the dark.

Just a game, I tried to tell myself. *It's nothing, just a game.*

I told myself that I could play this game, that I could pretend, just like Allie had pretended.

Askew held the shining knife blade before me.

'Do you abandon life?'

'I abandon life.'

'Do you truly wish to die?'

'I truly wish to die.'

He rested his hand on my shoulder. He drew me closer. I saw nothing but his eyes, heard nothing but his voice.

'This is no game,' he whispered, soft, soft.

'You will truly die,' he whispered. 'All you see and all you know will disappear. It is the end. You will be no more.'

He closed my eyes.

'This is Death,' he said.

And I knew no more.

I came to on the damp clay floor. My cheek was cold, icy. My limbs were stiff and sore. Only one of the candles still burned, a cold, meagre light. A demon from the wall glared down at me. I heard nothing. I twisted, turned, sat up, pressed my eyes, shook my head. I remembered nothing, just darkness, emptiness. Pain and stiffness in my bones. Frail muscles. Crawled on all fours to the steps, reached up to draw the door aside. Then I heard the voices: little high-pitched whispers, little giggles. I stared into the darkness of the den, saw nothing but the bones, the paintings, the carvings.

I rubbed my eyes.

'Who's there?' I whispered.

The giggling intensified.

I rubbed my eyes again, squinted, and then I saw them, skinny bodies in the flickering light. They hunched in the corners at the light's edge. They blended with the walls. They shifted and faded as I tried to focus on them. But I saw their goggling eyes, their blackened skin, heard their high-pitched giggles, and I knew that they were with me, the ancient pit children, down there in the darkness of Askew's den. They didn't stay. Gradually they disappeared, and I was alone.

I drew the door aside. There was only Askew left, hunched over beside Jax, facing the river, and Allie in the long grass chewing her thumb.

Askew stared. 'Well?' he said.

I couldn't speak. I shook my head. I just returned his gaze.

'You saw,' he said.

I turned away.

'You saw, Kit Watson,' he said again. 'And once you've seen, you'll keep on seeing more.'

I tottered to Allie. She stood up and held my arm, and watched me, and I saw the concern in her, the desire to protect me. We left Askew and began to walk together through the wilderness.

'Jeez, Kit,' she said. 'Thought you were never going to come out.'

I couldn't speak to her.

'Kit,' she said. 'Kit, man. Mr Watson.'

We walked on. I felt the strength coming back to me.

She kept staring at me.

'Kit,' she said. 'Kit.'

'It's all right,' I whispered. 'I'm all right.'

'What did he mean?' she said. 'What did he say you saw.'

I cast my eyes across the wilderness. I squinted, saw them again, the shifting skinny bodies at the edges of my vision. I heard their giggles, their whispers.

'I'll kill him,' she said. 'Cave man.' She made me stop. We stood together on the turf in the sun. 'Come on,' she said. 'Pull yourself together.'

I took long deep breaths, shook my head, tried to smile at her.

'You,' she said. 'Too innocent, that's your trouble. Drive me wild.' She squeezed my arm. We walked on. She took me towards the gate. 'Kit,' she kept saying. 'Kit, man. Kit.'

I looked again across the wilderness.

'You see them?' I whispered.

'See? See what?' She stared into my eyes. 'Kit, man. See what?'

I looked around again. There was nothing there. Just the ordinary world, the ordinary children playing there on the ordinary wilderness. The pit children had gone.

'Nothing,' I whispered. 'Nothing. I'm fine now.' I shook my head again, squeezed my eyes. Was it all a dream? 'I didn't pretend,' I told her.

'I know that, Kit. I can see that.'

I saw my mother at the window, gazing out.

'I'll have to go,' I said.

'You'll tell me some time, though?'

'Yes, Allie. I'll tell you what it was like to die in the den.'

We separated at the fence.

'I'll see you tomorrow, Kit,' she said. She didn't move.

'It really really happened, didn't it?' she said.

I nodded.

'You,' she said. 'You.'

I went inside.

'Where you been?' Mum said.

'Just down by the river, with Allie.'

She laughed. 'That lass,' she said.

I sat at the table and started to pick at some food. I stared out through the window, towards the children of Stoneygate playing between the houses and the river.

Grandpa watched me, as if I wasn't there.

Thirteen

Afternoon light poured through the classrom windows. Burning Bush smiled at us all as she read my tale. I kept my head down, felt my face beginning to flush.

'It's wonderful, Christopher,' she said, as she came to the end and laid the pages on the desk in front of her.

I heard a few of the others agreeing with her, heard a few sniggers. I glanced up and caught Allie looking at me from across the room. She grinned and put her tongue out, then she winked at me.

'And is it really true?' said Burning Bush. 'Did the pitmen really see the boy?'

'That's what he told me.'

She beamed.

'Well,' she said. 'You'll have to get him to tell you more tales if it produces work like this.' She held the story up to the class. 'It's another one for the wall, I think. Silky, by Christopher Watson.' She put it down and picked up someone else's story.

Annie Myers in front of me put her hand up.

'Yes, Ann?'

'Can we really call it Kit's story if it's one he got from his grandfather?'

Burning Bush nodded. 'Good question. Yes, we can. All writers write down stories they've heard. Writers have always done it. The greatest writers, like Chaucer, or Shakespeare. It's how stories work. They move from person to person, get passed down through the generations. And each time they're written down they're a little different. I'm sure, for instance, that Kit added a few touches of his own to his grandfather's tale. Yes, Kit?'

'Yes.'

She smiled.

'So stories change and evolve. Like living things. Yes, just like living things.'

Ann turned round to me. 'Don't think I didn't like it, Kit,' she said. 'Just wondered, that's all. Thought it was great.'

'And of course,' said Burning Bush, 'the spoken story and the written story are very different ways of telling.' She pondered. 'Get him to tell you more,' she said. 'And I wonder – might he be willing to come here and tell one of his stories to us all?'

'You've recovered, then?' Allie said as we walked back home.

I smiled and shrugged. 'Yeah.'

'What happened?'

'Dunno. Nothing.' I looked at her. 'I didn't pretend.'

'I know that.'

We walked on. I had my hand in my pocket. I held Grandpa's ammonite in my palm.

'You don't remember anything?'

'Nothing, Allie.'

'No devils, no angels?'

'Nothing.'

'Jeez, Kit.'

I cast my mind back to the game. There really was nothing to remember. It had just been total darkness that I'd entered. The darkness behind Askew's eyes. The darkness of a pit. Only when I came out of it had there been anything to remember, and then the ancient children had faded as if they were a dream.

We walked on.

'What is it?' she said. 'Hypnotism or something?'

'Dunno.'

'Would you do it again?'

'Dunno.'

She walked slowly.

'Jeez, Kit,' she said. 'Not pretending. Everybody else does. I'm sure they do.'

We walked on.

'Was it scary? Like dreaming? Like being asleep?'

'Dunno, Allie. It was like nothing. It was like being nothing.'

'Jeez,' she whispered. 'Jeez.'

'There was something when I came out of it,' I said.

'Something?'

'Yes.' I looked down. I was certain she would scoff at me. 'There were children, lots of them. Children from the Stoneygate of long ago. But when I look back now I think they were just a dream.'

She just looked at me. 'Jeez, Kit,' she said. 'Like the boy in your story, Silky.'

'Yes, but lots of them.'

'You've seen them again?'

'No, Allie.' I stared across the wilderness, squinted. 'No. They were just a kind of dream.'

We came in silence to the gate. Grandpa was in a deck-chair in the garden, grinning at us. He had his battered sunhat on.

'It's that bad lass!' he called. 'That little imp that drove me old missus wild!'

He waved us in. 'Said it was the wildest bairn she'd ever known,' he said. He laughed and patted Allie's arm. 'The wildest and the loveliest. That's what she said.'

Allie giggled and wagged her finger like Grandma used to, spoke just like she used to.

'Allie Keenan, you'll drive me round the twist and round the bend and up the pole, I'm telling you you will!'

'Hahaha!' said Grandpa. 'That's her! That's her to a tee!' He shook his head and grinned into the past. 'Give us a song,' he said. 'Go on, hinny, let's have a song.' He winked at me. 'Should've heard this one singing as a littl'un. Sang like an angel, danced like the devil.'

Allie thought.

'You join in,' she said. 'Like she used to.'

'Gan on, then. You start it, pet.'

Allie took a deep breath, started, and he quickly joined in.

Wisht, lads, had yer gobs
An I'll tell yez all an aaful story,
Wisht, lads, had yer gobs
An I'll tell ye aboot the worm . . .

They sang and sang, leaned close together, swayed together, moved in time to the music that joined them one to one.

Fourteen

I did want to ask Grandpa to come into school to tell his tales. The trouble was, we were already worried that tales were coming to an end. It was Mum that noticed first. It seemed nothing, just little moments when we lost him. Once she told us to look out for it, though, we got to easily see when it was happening. We'd be eating a meal together, the four of us, talking, joking, telling each other about the day we'd had, and suddenly it would be like he wasn't with us for a while. He'd stop talking and listening. He wouldn't touch his food. His eyes'd go blank and dull and he'd just stare out across us. Sometimes it was just the tiniest flicker of time when he lost attention, sometimes it lasted a few seconds. Sometimes Mum had to lean across and tap him on the arm.

'Dad,' she'd say. 'Dad.' And he'd come back to us again, with his eyes all confused.

'Eh?' he's say. 'Eh?'

'Where you been, Dad?'

He'd blink his eyes, he'd look at us like he was seeing us for the first time, he'd shake his head.

We'd all smile at him, dead gentle. Mum'd rub his arm. And he'd sigh and his eyes would clear and we'd all laugh about it together.

'Been off with the fairies?' she'd say.

'Aye,' he'd whisper. 'Aye, that's the style, eh?'

And we'd all laugh again, and start to eat and talk again, and try not to let the fear show in our eyes.

Some days it was worse, long periods when he just sat on the sofa or at the table with his body slumped and the blankness in his eyes. One day I sat with Mum after school in the living room and we watched him: two minutes, three minutes, four minutes, and he went on with his eyes just dead and blank, staring, but like he was seeing nothing inside and nothing outside.

'Oh, dear,' Mum whispered. 'Poor soul.'

'Maybe he's just remembering,' I told her. 'Like he always did.'

'No, son,' she whispered. 'What he's doing is forgetting.'

And I said nothing more. I thought of the den, of knowing nothing, remembering nothing. I trembled as I watched him, lost in his darkness. I knew that what Mum said was true.

Fifteen

Early morning in the kitchen. The sun blazing in at the window, but clouds gathering from the direction of the sea. Grandpa at the table drinking tea. No one else there. I hurried my breakfast, checked my bag. Everything was in there: last night's homework, pen case, books, packed lunch. I checked my pocket, fingered the heavy hard ammonite that rested there.

'It's like following Silky, son.'

I turned to him and touched his hand.

'That's what it's like. I've been sitting here, trying to work out what it's like.'

I held him tighter. I watched and listened. I thought of the way he turned his face to the sun, the way he strode through the hawthorn lanes, the way he belted out his songs and told his ancient tales.

'It's like following him all alone along the darkest tunnel, along a tunnel you never knew existed, way past all the other men. It's like getting to where you think Silky is and finding nothing there. Just darkness. Just nothing. And you can't move, and you don't know how to get back. And the more you stand there the more the darkness comes into you, till there's nothing but the darkness, and you don't see nothing, you don't hear nothing, you don't know nothing, you don't remember nothing.'

I held on to him, as if my grip might keep him here with us forever in the world of light. He took my hand in both of his, sipped his tea and smiled.

'That's right,' he told me. 'Cling on to me, boy. Keep me with you.'

'I do think I understand,' I said. 'You don't see anything. You don't hear anything.'

'Nothing.'

'You don't remember anything.'

'Nothing. Nothing to remember.'

'And you're not scared till you come back.'

'Scared to find out that you've been away at all. Scared to think you'll be going away again. But when you're there . . . Nothing.'

He shrugged and smiled again.

'And coming back's like being found again. Like the men coming through the tunnels with their lamps and calling out to you.'

He shook his head again.

'Old man's troubles. They're not for lads like you, however much you think you understand,' he said. 'But I want to find a way to help you see what's happening. If I can help you, be less scary for you, eh?'

'Yes,' I whispered.

He reached across and gently stroked my tears away with his fingertips.

'No need for that,' he whispered. 'I've done my time, as you'll do yours.'

And he winked at me.

'That mate of yours,' he said. 'That lass. She's the one. One that's filled with light and life. Keep near to her, boy.'

Sixteen

I hardly slept that night. Children giggled and whispered all around me. I stared out and saw dark cloud hanging low over Stoneygate. Hardly a light to be seen. Grandpa groaned behind the wall. I tried to pray for him but the words were dead and empty on my tongue. Next morning he wouldn't wake. It seemed as if he'd never wake. Mum sat by his bed with a mug of tea cooling in her hands.

'Dad,' she whispered. 'Come on, Dad.' I said I'd stay with her but she snapped at me. 'Go to school. Do your duty. Get to school.'

I ran through drizzle to the gates. The clouds stayed all day. Rain flooded down the windows during lessons. All day I thought of him lying there in darkness, in nothingness.

In Geography, Dobbs yelled at Allie for taking no notice of him.

'You may think tectonic plates have nothing to do with you, Miss Keenan!' he yelled. 'But that's just because the plates in your own skull have yet to join up with each other.

You're an infant world, girl. You're semi-formed. You're a tectonic gap.'

I saw the tears in her eyes, her clenched fists, saw how she'd like to rip him limb from limb.

We sat together in the corridor at break and listened to the rain hammering on the roof. I wanted to find a way of telling her about my Grandpa, but she was filled with spite. All she did was stamp the floor, squeeze her eyes, spit her breath out.

'Hate this place,' She hissed. 'Hate it and everybody in it. Maybe I won't even wait till they let me go. I'll take myself off early. Runaway, vagabond, make my own life.' She pinched my arm. 'You could come with me, Kit. Take a bag and set off wandering. Me and you together.'

'Eh?' I said.

She laughed, her mouth twisted.

'Eh? Eh? You? Course you wouldn't. And even if you did you'd drive me wild. Eh? Eh? Eh?'

I bared my teeth at her. 'You,' I said. 'Dobbs is right. All you think about is you, you, bloody you.'

And she stamped off down the corridor.

Then the bell went and I headed down to French. I passed Askew being yelled at by Chambers, the deputy head. Askew was a lout, he said, an imbecile, a disgrace to the school. Askew lounged against the wall with his head down, just taking it all. He lifted his eyes and sneered at me as I passed.

'Mr Resurrection, eh?' he muttered.

'What was that?' said Chambers. 'What was that you said to me?'

'Nowt,' said Askew, and I heard the deep tedium in his voice. 'Nowt. Just nowt.'

Then French, and Maths, and sandwiches that tasted like cardboard in my mouth, and snappy teachers and miserable kids and the rain pouring pouring down. Everything inside and outside just a blur. Just wanting to get back out and get back home again and see how Grandpa was. Kept gripping the ammonite in my fist. How long had it been down there, in the earth, till it was found again? How long did anything have to be in the dark before it was found again?

Then English, and Burning Bush wanting to make a fuss about the story again. Maybe we should get some illustrations, she said. Maybe we should make a coloured cover for it. She smiled at me. What did I think?

'Aye,' I muttered. 'Anything.'

She looked at me. 'Good,' she said. 'Maybe we could talk about it when the lesson's over.'

'Yes. Anything,' I said.

And she talked about Shakespeare and Chaucer while the rain came to an end at last and the clouds began to break and weak beams of sunlight shone on to the sodden wilderness.

'So,' she said, when the others had gone. 'Illustrations. Any idea who we could get to do them for us?'

I shrugged.

'John Askew, maybe,' I said.

She raised her eyes.

'He's a talented artist,' she said.

I nodded.

'And a friend of yours?'

I nodded.

She looked at me.

'Is everything all right, Kit?'

'Yes, thanks.'

I looked out, saw the others gathering at the gate. Allie there, scowling.

Burning Bush started on about the cover, how it would be great if we scanned an illustration into the computer, put the title above it, my name beneath it, just like a proper book.

I stood there, let her go on. Outside, Askew and Jax disappeared over the edge of the wilderness.

'I've got to go,' I said.

'Sorry?'

'Got to go.'

'I thought this might be interesting for you.'

'It is. But . . .'

She caught my arm as I tried to leave.

'Christopher. What's going on with you? What is it, Kit?'

'Nowt,' I spat. 'Bloody nowt.'

And I shook my head, pulled away, lifted my bag, just left her there, hurried out. Why didn't I hurry home to Grandpa? Why did I rush to play the game called Death instead? The questions stormed inside me as I stood there at the gate with the others. I saw Burning Bush watching from a window. What you looking at? I wanted to yell at her. What's it got to do with you? I told myself, *Go home. Go home.* But I stood there sullen and silent with my eyes downcast, held back by the terror of what I might find if I did go home, and driven to the darkness that my Grandpa knew, driven to the darkness that I knew I'd find again in the den that day.

Allie didn't look at me. We set off across the soaked ground. Great pools of water in the grass. Water vapour rising and drifting white beneath the weak rays of the sun. Cold breeze coming from the river. Clouds low and grey, scudding slowly over the wilderness. Feet splashing, trousers soaked, not a word spoken. The long wet grass. Standing there in silence. Jax's bark. Askew's hand. The door drawn back. We go down, into the drenched den. Crouch with feet in the shallow pool that covers the floor. Look across at Allie's eyes. You, they say. You drive me wild. You're on your own. Look at my name, Christopher Watson, carved into the wall, into the long list of the dead. Sip the water, smoke the cigarette, watch the spinning knife. Me, not me, me, not me, me, not me . . . I know that it will be me again. The knife stops, pointing at my feet. I take Askew's hand, kneel in the pool, crouch in the pool, hear Askew's whispered words, stare into his eyes, feel his touch. This is not a game. You will truly die. This is death. Collapse into the pool. Darkness. Nothing.

Seventeen

Then the end of it all.

I'm deep in darkness, then I hear my name, time and again.

'Kit! Kit! Kit! Kit!'

Light shines in on me. Hands grip my shoulders, shake me. Water splashes across my face.

'Kit! Kit! Kit!'

I open my eyes.

Burning Bush crouches at my side. She's kneeling in the pool, her red hair's burning in the light that pours down into the den.

'Kit,' she says, more softly. 'Kit.' She strokes my face, puts her hands beneath my shoulders, begins to pull me from the floor.

Beyond her, all the faces stare down from the edge of the den.

'What *is* this?' whispers Burning Bush.

I can't speak. I see Allie leaning in towards us, desperation on her face.

'Don't wake him!' she yells. 'Don't wake him, stupid Burning Bush!'

Tears are pouring from her eyes. 'Don't wake him!' she yells.

Burning Bush lifts me further from the floor.

'Come on,' she says. 'Come on. Wake up, Kit Watson.'

She glares up at the faces. 'What *is* this?' she shouts. 'What's been going on?'

The faces disappear. Only Allie stays, staring in, weeping.

'Come and *help* us,' says Burning Bush.

And Allie clambers in. The two of them haul me to my feet. My legs are leaden. I remember nothing, just darkness, nothingness. I hear whispering, giggling. I see skinny bodies shifting at the edges of my vision. I turn and turn my head, trying to see them true.

'Kit!' says Burning Bush. 'Come on, Kit! Snap out of it.'

They help me up towards the entrance and out into the light.

I scan the wilderness. Children are scattering away across the grass towards their homes.

Burning Bush names them as they flee.

'Daniel Sharkey,' she says. 'Robert Carr, Louise McCall . . .'

We rest on the grass. Burning Bush's face is set in anger.

'What *is* this?' she demands.

Allie strokes my face, my hair, my shoulders.

A dark thick-set figure and a dog move away along the riverbank.

'And John Askew,' whispers Burning Bush. 'I might have known. John Askew.'

Part Two

WINTER

One

Next day, all but one of us stood in Chamber's office. He had Burning Bush's report in front of him, and the list of our names. He watched us, as if he were mystified, as if we were strangers to him. He said he was troubled to see such leanings to darkness in those who were so young and who had such bright futures before them. 'What am I to make of it?' he said. 'How can you explain it?' Outside, frost had formed on the wilderness. I peered out past Chamber's confused face. Askew was out there, a black figure on the white ground, walking heavily through the white misty air. Bundled up in heavy clothes, black woollen hat pulled down over his head, sketch pad under his arm, Jax by his side.

'Watson!' snapped Chambers. He peered into my eyes. 'Can't you even concentrate on what I'm saying, boy?'

I tore my eyes away from Askew. The others told the story of the game: the way we played it, the way we died, the way we came back to life again. Chambers asked about Askew, and it was agreed that yes, it had been Askew's game and Askew's den, and Bobby went on to cry and say that we couldn't help ourselves, that there was evil in Askew. That he had enticed us and threatened us. That we were under his spell. Daniel and Louise nodded their heads at that.

'Yes,' they whispered. 'We couldn't help ourselves. Askew is evil. We were under his spell.'

They hung their heads and said they would never go near Askew again.

Allie clicked her tongue.

'Yes, Alison?' said Chambers.

'Well,' she said. 'It's nonsense. It was just a stupid game, that's all. And Askew's just a lout. A cave man. Evil, huh!'

Chambers pondered.

'Be careful,' he whispered. 'There is such a thing as evil in the world. And it may well be that those who doubt it are those at most risk from it.'

He scribbled in his notebook.

'Christopher?' he said. 'You're very quiet.'

I shrugged. 'No,' I said. 'He isn't evil. There's good in everyone. There's good in Askew. He's just different from the rest of us. And it was just a game.'

Chambers shook his head and went on writing.

'You're just children.' he said. 'Innocents. It is our duty to protect you. You have to understand that there are people who can lead us into great danger.'

He looked at our faces one by one. He said the board of governors would decide what action should be taken against us.

'I think that our Mr Askew will be taking his leave of us,'

he said. 'Make sure you don't follow him into the wilderness.'

As we left his office I caught Bobby staring at me.

'What you looking at?' I said.

'She woke you up,' he said.

Allie clicked her tongue.

'A living death,' said Bobby. 'That's what he said you'd have. Living death.'

Allie got him by the throat.

'You're a worm,' she said. 'D'you know that? If anybody's evil or living dead, it's you.'

And she shoved him away.

The days passed. Askew was expelled. We were warned about our future conduct. We were warned not to inflame the minds of the younger children in school with stories of what had gone on. We stood at the edge of the school field and watched the bulldozer heading across the wilderness to fill in the den.

Burning Bush called me back as I was leaving her class one day.

'You're all right, now, Kit?' she said.

'Yes, thanks, Miss.'

'You had me terrified, you know.'

'I know. I'm sorry, Miss.'

'An imagination like yours is a powerful thing,' she said. 'But it can be overwhelming, especially in one so young.'

'Yes, Miss.'

'Be careful with it, eh?'

'Yes, Miss.'

'Stick to writing stories with it, eh?'

'Yes, Miss.'

She smiled.

'No need to act the stories out, Kit. The words are enough.'

They were gentle at home. They talked about Grandma's death and Grandpa's illness. They said the main thing was that the game was over now, and that awful John Askew was gone. Dad even laughed about it. He talked about the old game of dancing round the graveyard memorial in the dark.

'Scared ourselves half to death with tales and visions. The strange thing was, we *wanted* to be terrified. It was like we were *driven* to play the stupid game. Taken further, suppose it could have ended up like yours did.'

He shook his head.

'Kids' games, eh? Still, it's over now and lessons learned. You'll not be up to anything like that again, eh?'

I shook my head.

'No.'

They tried to keep the tale of Askew's den from Grandpa, but he got the gist of it. He came in and sat behind me on the bed while I was reading.

'Bit of bother?'

'Aye,' I said.

'It'll pass. That's the great thing you can say about everything – it'll pass. Want to tell me about it?'

I shrugged.

'Don't think so,' I said. 'It was just a game, that's all. And it went wrong.'

'Fair enough, son.'

He peered over my shoulder. 'What's the homework this time?'

'Geography. How all the continents were once one single continent.'

'Is that right, now?'

'Yes. It was called Pangaea. Then the continents broke away and separated.'

I showed him the map of how the world was all those millions of years ago, how the earth could twist and tear, how it was endlessly changing, endlessly reforming itself.

He smiled. 'You'll go a long way, lad.' He got up to go out again. 'Mind you,' he said. 'Hope you're not keeping it from me cos you think an old bloke like me wouldn't understand.'

I turned to him. 'No, Grandpa,' I said.

I didn't tell him that he'd be able understand it more than any other.

Two

Winter deepened in Stoneygate. Hard frost on the wilderness, ice on the pools there, white flowers and ferns on the windowpanes. Grandpa moved in and out of his darkness. Some days his eyes were bright and his singing echoed gently through the house. Other days he was lost to us, staring through the wintry world with vacant eyes. Allie came for me each morning. She stood on the step with a red bobble hat on, green scarf, red coat, white plumes of breath rising from her lips. On his good days, Grandpa would grin out of the kitchen at her, call her the little bad lass.

'Fairy Queen!' he'd call. 'Red and green should never be seen, except on the back of a fairy queen!'

And Allie would laugh and say, 'Come on, Mr Watson. Let's get away from that bad old man!'

The air like ice, stinging. Frost and ice on the pavements. Our voices hanging in the air, muffled by the cold, going nowhere. The clack of Allie's little heels. The voices and footsteps of others around us, heading to school. A bunch of young ones used to watch us at the gate. They whispered together, deepening the rumours of what had really gone on down there. Suddenly Allie would jump at them, hiss, bare her teeth, raise her fingers like claws, and they would scatter, giggling, loving the fright.

'And I'll be good today again,' she used to say, straightening her back and raising her head as we approached the doors. 'Just like yesterday, and the yesterday before.' She giggled. 'Miss Perfect,' she said. 'Yes sir, Mr Dobbs. No sir, Mr Dobbs. The Great Rift Valley. Really? How fascinating, sir. Please tell us more.'

We moved easily through the days. Listening, taking notes, answering questions, asking questions. Condensation streamed down the windows. The sun outside trickled through the mist. Frost relented in the mornings, took hold again each afternoon. And Allie really said those things: Yes, sir, Mr Dobbs. No, sir, Mr Dobbs. She said that the great Rift Valley was fascinating. And Mr Dobbs raised his eyes and smiled at her.

'Well, Miss Keenan, so good to see you're continuing to turn the new leaf. There's hope for us yet.'

'Jeez, Kit,' she said as we walked home again in the fading light. 'Isn't it boring being good?'

Often we saw Askew looming through the dusk with Jax, as he crossed and re-crossed the wilderness.

'He must get freezing, Kit,' said Allie. 'He'll turn to ice.'

'It is boring,' I said. 'But maybe we've had enough excitement for the time being.'

'Hope it comes again,' she whispered, and she tilted her

head back, breathed a long fast plume of breath into the darkening air.

Three

Another early morning. More frost and mist on the wilderness. Dawn breaking. Winter deepening. It was weeks now since the final events in the den, weeks of calm and quiet, just broken by the fears caused by Grandpa's lapses. We'd been told that some day, maybe soon, he'd have to be taken away from us, that we wouldn't be able to care for him any longer.

We turned the heating up high now, and flowers and ferns didn't form on the window panes. The world out there was distorted and confused by a thousand beads of water, by sudden trickles of water.

Grandpa was at the table with his morning tea, wrapped in memory, smiling gently into the past. His song trickled from his lips.

> '*When I was young and in me prime,*
> *Eh, aye, I could hew . . .*'

Then he blinked and lifted his head. 'There was one year,' he said. 'Cold as Hell. Wonderful. Ice that stayed for months. Deep snow in the lanes and fields. Even the river froze. Yeah, froze from bank to bank. D'you believe it? True as I'm sitting here, boy.' He smiled at me. 'Yep. Wonderful. Days as bright as Heaven when the sun shone. And at night, all the frost and snow and ice shining under the stars. Glistening nights!'

Mum came in and shook her head.

'That old tale,' she said. 'And the day you walked with Johnny Sharkey and Col Gullane right to the other side and back again?'

'Ha, you've heard it before, eh, pet? Once or twice? Mind you, with much slipping and sliding on the way.'

'And there were snowmen standing in the middle of the river, and skaters . . .'

'Ha. All of that. All of that. Cold as Hell for months and months.'

He smiled into himself again. Mum winked at me, touched him gently on the shoulder, leaned forward and kissed him softly on the head, then went upstairs.

'Mind you,' he said. 'Lethal, too, specially when Spring come. One lad drowned when the ice began to melt down Bill Quay way. Went through the ice, sledge and all, poor soul. Put an end to it. Watched the gap growing at the centre, the river running free again.' He pondered. 'Grand days, grand days. But aye, Spring was dangerous.'

The letterbox in the hall clicked.

'Post!' he said.

Just one brown envelope lay on the mat. 'Kit' was written on it in clumsy writing. No stamp, no address. I slowly tore it open.

It was a charcoal drawing, deep black. I saw the tunnels of

the pit, the men bending forward to the coal, the cones of light from their lamps. Behind them stood a glistening fair-headed boy in shorts and boots. His head was turned, he looked out of the drawing. He was poised as if to begin running. Silky.

On the back of the drawing, in the clumsy writing. It said: 'for your story.'

I turned it round so that it faced Grandpa.

'Silky!' he said. 'Just as he was.' He stared down into the black. 'Aye. Just as he was.'

'It's John Askew's,' I said.

'He would know. From his own grandfather. Caught him dead right. Little mischief.'

I looked out of the window, saw Askew far out there, heading away, distorted by the water on the pane.

'He read the story I did for school,' I said. 'Drew it for that.'

'Clever lad.' Grandpa looked at me. 'Thought he was off the team, though,' he said.

I shrugged. 'Aye. I suppose.'

Mum came in, lifted the drawing, said how good it was. Then realised. 'John Askew?'

'Yes.'

'Hope he doesn't think he can buy favour with this kind of thing.' She dropped the drawing back on to the table.

'Ah, well,' said Grandpa. He grinned. He reached down and touched the glistening boy with his fingertip. 'Little Silky, eh?'

I went upstairs and put it in my room, on the wall beside the drawing of me. Then Mum was calling.

'Kit! Allie's here!'

Four

That day after school I went out alone, climbed the fence. There were dozens of kids playing in the gathering dark. There was a slide on a bare patch of ground. Someone had brought a lantern down. They slid through its pale glow, clashed into each other, went sprawling, laughed and squealed.

'Kit!' someone yelled. 'Come and play, Kit!'

Then screamed: 'Aaaaaaa! Hahaha!'

I waved and walked on. The frosted grass crunched and crackled under my feet. The houselights from the opposite bank shimmered on the slow river. Stars brightened as the dark came on. No moon. I looked down and was certain I saw ice forming there at the river's edge. Cold enough, I though. Bitter cold.

I closed my eyes, saw Grandpa as a boy, slipping and sliding on the ice. I smiled to myself, then heard a whispering, a tiny giggling nearby. Opened my eyes, saw nothing.

'Who's there?' I whispered.

I stared into the dark, squinted, heard the whispering again.

'Who's there?'

Then there came a sudden growl, a mutter.

'Down! Leave him!'

'Askew?' I whispered.

He lurched out of the dark, the dog beside him blacker than the night. He stood yards away from me. My breath quickened, heart thudded. I reached into my pocket, gripped the ammonite.

'I got your picture,' I said.

He grunted something.

'It's brilliant,' I said.

He held the dog by its collar. Its white teeth glistened in the dark.

'I know it is,' he said.

'I put it on my wall, Askew.'

'You,' he said. 'Bloody you.'

'Me what?'

'You. Mr Perfect. Mr Butter-Wouldn't-Melt.'

'Eh?'

'Eh? Eh? It was you that spoiled it, Mr Teacher's Pet.'

'Eh?'

'It was you that brought her running.'

He stepped closer, gripped my collar.

'What's it about you that gets everybody running to protect you?'

We watched each other.

'Don't know what you mean,' I said.

He growled, and the dog growled at his side.

'He'd tear you limb from limb,' he said.

'Askew,' I said, exasperated with him.

'You,' he said. 'You and that stupid pretty thing.'

I tugged away.

'Get off me,' I said. 'You're being . . .'

He gripped me tighter, so tight I could hardly breathe. He glared, and his eyes glittered with reflected light.

'What d'you want?' I whispered.

'From you? Nothing. Nowt.'

But he held me close.

'Kit Watson,' he whispered. 'Kit Watson, aged thirteen. What's it like?'

'Eh?'

'Eh? Eh? Living death. What's it like?'

'Like nothing,' I said. 'It's nonsense.'

'Aye?'

He grunted again. He wanted to hurt me with his grip, wanted to frighten me with his eyes. But I could feel that his grip was also a way of clinging to me, that his eyes were also filled with yearning. It was Askew who needed someone to protect him, Askew who needed love.

'You could be something, you know,' I said.

He sneered.

'You could,' I said. 'Your drawing's brilliant. You're throwing yourself away. You're being stupid.'

The dog growled, strained against his grip. We watched each other in silence.

'Watch what you say,' he said. 'Just watch it, Kit.'

I heard wordless whispering around us again, an intake of breath. At the edge of my vision, in the darkness, children crouched and watched us. I turned my eyes from Askew, peered past him, squinted.

He laughed, low, guttural.

'Aye,' he said. 'There's them that see and them that don't. You're closer to me than you think, Kit Watson.'

'I know that,' I said. I met his eyes again. 'We're closer than anyone could think,' I said. 'And I know we could be friends.'

He pushed me away at the word.

'Friends!' he hissed. 'Bloody friends!'

He moved away with the dog.

'Yes,' I whispered after him. 'John Askew, aged thirteen, friend of Christopher Watson, aged thirteen.'

I stood there, listening, squinting, searching the darkness, then hurried home, and there were skinny children all around.

Five

'Jeez, Kit. It's such a drag, man.'

'Come on,' I said. 'We'll do it together.'

Allie slumped in her chair and sighed.

We were working on Pangaea, on the kitchen table. We had to show how it was formed from all the continents that we have now. I stared at the maps, saw how the coasts of Africa and America could be slotted into each other, how India could fit tight against Africa. I read how the movement of continents and countries away from each other continues.

'It is,' I said. 'It's easy.'

I started to cut out the continents from the map so that we could fit them together.

Allie clicked her tongue, picked her nails, sighed.

'Who wants to know?' she said. 'Who wants to go a million million years into the past?'

I just went on, cutting out, fitting together.

'Mr Watson,' she said. She drummed her fingers on the table. 'Mr Watson heading back into the past. Mr Watson in his element.'

'Stop it, Allie.'

'That's very good,' she said, acting Mr Dobbs as I went on. 'Excellent, Christopher. And did you realise that the continents continue to move away from each other, perhaps as slowly as our fingernails grow? You knew that? Very good, Christopher. Such a fine pupil. Perhaps some of you others should follow Christopher's example. What's that, Christopher? Ah, you wish to be a geography teacher yourself some day? Excellent. Excellent. We should have a proper chat some time. I'll give you the benefit of my experience. Allie Keenan! Stop dreaming, girl! Get some work done. Yes, sir, Mr Dobbs. Of course, Mr Dobbs. Pangaea, eh? How very very fascinating.'

She giggled. 'Jeez, Kit. what a drag, eh?'

Pangaea was made. I looked at it, all the continents together.

'Amazing,' I said. 'You think the earth's solid and fixed, but then you find out something like this.'

'Quite amazing, Mr Watson.'

'Anyway, it's done.'

'Thank God for that. Dobbs'll be delighted, eh?'

Allie started putting her books back into her bag. 'D'you never wish it was all just over and done with?'

'Eh?'

'Eh? School and books and homework. So you can get out in the world and get going properly.'

'Suppose so.'

Allie grinned.

'Is that bad little lass still here?' called Grandpa from the living room.

'Yes!' she shouted. 'She's still in here!'

'Driving me grandson round the bend and up the pole, I bet!'

'Aye! And round the twist and all!'

'Hahaha! Good lass! Good bad lass!'

Allie giggled again and twisted her face.

'I do, though,' she said. 'It's all such a drag, man.'

She stood up and slung her bag over her shoulder. 'Tomorrow morning?' she said.

'Tomorrow morning.'

Allie dropped her head forward, stood like someone stupid, nodded her head up and down, slowly grunted,

'Tomorrow . . . tomorrow . . . tomorrow . . . tomorrow.'

She was on her way out when we heard a sudden crash from next door, Mum's scream of terror.

'Dad!' she yelled. 'Dad! Oh, Dad!'

Six

He was slumped on the floor, head twisted back against the sofa. Face grey, eyes staring. Mum kneeling over him.

'Dad,' she whispered. 'It's all right, Dad. Stay calm. You'll be all right.'

My father was on the phone.

'Come on!' he said. 'Answer, answer!'

He saw me standing there, held his hand up. 'It's okay, son. He'll be all right. Come on, answer!'

I turned to Allie. She was in the doorway.

'Kit!' she whispered.

'Answer!' said Dad. 'Answer!'

Allie stared, and tears poured from her eyes, just like when she looked down into the den.

Seven

Silky came that night, long after the doctor had gone, long after Grandpa had been put to bed, long after I'd come to bed myself, long after the moon shone in through my window. Long after the moon had been blotted out and the snow began to fall, long after I'd tried to sleep and couldn't sleep and simply watched the snowflakes thicken on my windowsill.

Just a glimpse, from the corner of my eye. A shimmering like silk. I caught my breath. 'Who's there?' I whispered.

Nothing. Then again, nothing but a flickering. Nothing. I closed my eyes, saw the boy running away from me, glistening as he headed down the tunnel.

'There he is!' I called. 'After him! After him!'

I ran. Endless tunnels, heading further and further into the earth. Kept thinking I'd lost him, then saw him again. Just a glimpse, then gone. I followed, lost him, saw him, lost him. A little blond boy in shorts and boots. I kept on running into the endless dark but he was nowhere. Then again.

'There he is! There he is!'

He stood, head turned back to me, watching. Our eyes met. I gasped. I knew he was waiting for me, that he was leading me. He ran again, into the endless deep dark, nothing to be seen but his flickering before me, nothing to be heard but the thundering of my heart and and the gasping of my breath and the thumping of my feet. We ran an age, a million years. Far into the earth through secret unknown tunnels, a boy in front and a boy behind and darkness all around. And then a final flickering, and he was gone for good. Where was I? Deep inside the earth, deep inside the dark, alone. I stretched my hands out, inched forward, seeking a way out. Tiptoed forward, feet on the hard earth. Nothing, nothing to be seen. Then touched him, the man standing there beside me. Touched the shoulders, the face, the icy cheek, the open eyes. 'Grandpa,' I whispered. No answer. He was dead still, dead stiff. 'Grandpa.' I moved in close, put my arms around him. 'Grandpa. It's all right, Grandpa. Stay calm. It'll be all right.'

I held him tight. I held him tight for hours, for a million years, till at last we heard the footsteps in the tunnel, saw the distant light of the lamps, heard the voices of the men who'd come to find us. And Grandpa sighed and shook his head.

'Here they are,' he whispered. 'We're okay, son. Here they are.'

I opened my eyes to dawn. Snow lay thick on the windowsill. Great flakes drifted across the panes.

'Grandpa,' I whispered.

I pressed my cheek to the wall. I heard him moving in his bed, then his frail voice:

'*When I was young, and in me pri-ime . . .*'

Eight

Snow. Not a breath of wind. The flakes tumbled thickly from the low white sky, filled the gardens and lanes, rested thick on the rooftops, carpeted the wilderness. Snowmen appeared: coaly eyes, carrot noses, pebble-studded grins. The slides lengthened and widened. Parents rushed across the snow, pulling squealing children on sledges and plastic trays and binliners.

Each morning we woke to a brilliant new layer. It was wonderful to be the first across the fence each morning, to stamp the first fresh footprints there. It was great to trudge with Allie through it on our way to school, to hear her giggles muffled by the dead still snow-padded air. We made huge light balls of it, heard them thump softly on to fence posts and house walls, slung them at the others who walked around us. Snowballs everywhere, arching up into the misty air and down with a thump to the world again.

Allie danced across the snow in her brilliantly-coloured clothes, kicked a storm of white around her, grabbed my arm and tugged me and made me join in with her. We fell down with our legs and arms askew and printed the shapes of our bodies in it. We lifted our faces and opened our mouths and felt the single flakes melting gently on our tongues and laughed at each other and danced again. Our hands stung and our cheeks stung and even our hearts stung with the joy of it.

Even Dobbs joined in with the excitement of it. He put Pangaea aside. He told us about the Ice Ages, when the great glaciers crept down from the North, scouring the earth, forcing valleys into the greatest mountains. He told us about our ancestors, who moved southwards as the cold intensified, as the world around them froze. A brilliant white world, he said. A world of ice.

Burning Bush talked of how they sheltered in caves as they moved, how they gathered in terror around magical fires in there. Maybe this was how stories started, she said.

'Imagine them there, crouched around the fire in the smoke. They painted pictures of beasts on the walls, huge mammoths and bison, the tigers and bears that brought such terror to them. They painted little figures of themselves, little fragile men and women and children in a massive terrifying world. Imagine one of them, the storyteller. He wears animal skins. His hair is shaggy, his skin is blackened by smoke. He holds a burning torch. "Listen," he tells them, and they all lean closer to the fire, wide-eyed, staring at him, all agog. He casts the torch across the paintings on the wall, and the beasts, the terrifying world, the tiny men and women and children flash before their eyes. "Listen," he says, "and I'll tell you the story of the boldest of us all, his endless quest across the ice, his struggle with The Bear, his vision of The Sun God. His name was Lak . . ." '

Burning Bush paused and looked at us.

'That's your story for this week,' she said. 'The first sentence: *His name was Lak.*'

I lifted my pen and pondered.

His name was Lak . . . I wrote

Nine

Evening. The first break in the clouds for days. I climbed the fence. The sky was thick with stars. I stared up and found the Great Bear and Orion the Hunter. The flashing lights of an aeroplane moved beneath them. A shooting star streaked down towards the river. The snow was crisp, its surface brittle and icy, crackling as I walked. Many built fires out here now. They gathered logs, wooden boxes, palettes, lit them, sat in little groups around them, roasted potatoes in the embers, told jokes and scared each other with tales of ghosts and monsters. All across the wilderness the fires glowed and hunched figures leaned towards them.

'Kit,' called one group as I passed by. A bunch of little ones, little shining eager faces. 'Come and tell us that story again, Kit.'

I laughed. 'Later,' I said.

Walked on, into the deeper darkness above the river, saw by the light of the stars and the opposite houselights that the ice was taking over, beginning to creep out from the river's edge. How long would it take for the ice from the edges to meet up and cover the river beneath? I hunched down and watched, and I heard again the tiny whispering all around me. I saw children shifting at the edges of my vision. I squinted and saw the skinny silhouettes, saw the round eyes catching the light from stars.

Maybe I knew he'd be there as well. There was no surprise when I heard him, when I saw him from the corner of my eye, hunched over, further along the bank.

'Down,' he whispered. 'Leave him.'

Silence. Just the gentle running of the river, a distant giggling, far behind.

'Askew,' I said.

Nothing. I moved closer to him. I spoke his name softly, as if he were an animal in pain: likely to attack, but desperately in need of comfort and love.

'Askew,' I whispered. 'Askew.'

He sighed, grunted something, pulled his collar close, yanked his woollen hat down. The dog stirred as I drew nearer.

'You'll catch your death,' I said.

He grunted again.

Silence.

'What do you do all day?' I said.

He clicked his tongue.

Silence.

'You seen the ice?' I said.

No answer.

'It covered the whole river once,' I said. 'They walked

from bank to bank. A boy drowned when it melted.'

Nothing.

'Askew?' I said.

He yanked his hat again.

'You'll catch your death,' I said.

'You,' he whispered. 'You, and that stupid pretty one.'

'What?' I said.

Nothing.

We watched the water and the ice. I felt the cold creeping into me, into my bones, saw the starlit eyes watching from the dark, heard the shallow breath, the whispers. Shuddered.

'I've done more stories,' I said. 'You could do pictures. We could be a team.'

Askew grunted.

'Team. Bloody team!'

'The other one you did was great,' I said.

He lowered his head, gazed down. I saw the starlight caught in the dog's eyes, in its teeth.

'Afterwards,' I said. 'I dreamed about it. I dreamed that I was with Silky.'

Long silence.

'That's the way of it,' he said. 'You draw what you dream. Then you dream what you draw.'

'That's the way with stories, too.'

Silence, just skinny bodies shifting in the darkness.

'You see them?' I whispered.

'Them?'

I squinted, saw them, black silhouettes within the dark,

starlight catching in their eyes, starlight glistening on their skin.

'Them,' I said.

Askew grinned, turned his face to the dark. The bodies crouched, stared. I heard the intake of their breath.

'There's more than them,' he whispered. 'There's things from further back. You'll come to see them with your dead eyes, Kit Watson.' He stepped closer. 'I was going to find you out here. I was going to bring you down here. Throw you in, or let Jax on you.'

'Askew, man. Why?'

'Why? Cos I was. Cos everything was fine till you came here. Cos you were the one that brought the teacher running. Cos you were the one that got the game ended and me chucked out.' He laughed.

'But mebbe it's better this way. Mebbe it's what I've always wanted. Mebbe you've done me a favour Kit Watson. Pushed me further out towards the dark.'

I heard how his breath shuddered as he breathed, how his body shuddered. Closer to him, I saw how he was growing, how he was thickening, how massive he was becoming.

'Why don't you go home?' I said. 'You'll freeze out here.'

Nothing.

'Heading out soon,' he whispered. 'Me and him. Getting out.'

'Where to?'

'Don't matter. Nowhere. Somewhere. They'll wake up, we'll be gone.'

'Askew, man,' I said.

Silence.

'I'll bring a story round,' I said. 'Like you brought the picture.'

He grunted.

I felt the ice deepening in my bones.

'I will,' I whispered.

'Silky,' he said.

'Eh?'

'Eh? That Silky. I see him too. He shows himself to both of us, Kit Watson.' He didn't turn, just stayed hunched, facing the river. 'You're closer to me than you think,' he said.

'I know that. I've said I know that. So we should get together more, eh?'

'Together! Aye, mebbe we will. But it'll be me that chooses the time and chooses the place and we'll see if Kit Watson's brave enough to really get together with John Askew.' Askew spat and turned away.

'It'll be in deep darkness,' he muttered. 'It'll be where there's nobody, just John Askew, Kit Watson, and many many of the dead.'

I watched him fade into the dark. I walked home, heard the distant whispering behind me. The snow crackled under my feet. The little ones had gone, the glowing embers of their fires left behind.

A shooting star streaked towards Stoneygate's heart.

Ten

His name was Lak. He was fourteen. He wore the skin of the bear he'd killed. Deerskin was wrapped around his feet. He gripped a stone axe that had once belonged to his grandfather. The baby, Dal, was wrapped against his chest. The dog Kali lay at his side. He squatted on the crag and gazed down to the river of ice below him. Ice was everywhere, in the valleys, in the cracks of stones, in fissures of the rock, in his hair, in his eyebrows. It covered the world: bare rock above, ice beneath. It glistened and gleamed in the morning sun. Lak narrowed his eyes against the glare. He peered across the world, searching for smoke rising, for a sign of humanity, of his lost family. He saw nothing, just the white ice, the dark rock, the great blue sky, the low yellow sun.

He called out: 'Ayeeeee!'

His voice came back to him from the ice and rock, it echoed and died away as it travelled down the valley:

'Ayeeeee! Ayeeeee! Ayeeeee!'

The dog lifted its head, stared out, ears pricked.

Lak laughed. 'It's only me,' he said. 'Me echoing forever on the ice.'

He reached into the bearskin, touched the baby, felt her swaddled close against his skin, felt her warm lips, her warm cheek.

'It will be fine,' he whispered. 'Keep calm, my love. It will all be fine.'

He crawled on the crag. He found the tiny thorny plants that grew sparsely there, the only things that grew now. He picked them, shoved them into his mouth, chewed, swallowed, twisted his face, spat. Bitter-tasting things. Sharp on the tongue, acid in the belly. He took a tiny blossom, the only sweet part of the plant, moistened it with saliva, held it to the baby's tongue. He felt her lick.

'Keep calm,' he whispered. 'Perhaps there will be berries this day.'

He held a plant on his palm for the dog. It licked, didn't eat, turned its hungry eyes forlornly to its master. Lak grunted, stroked the dog. 'Perhaps there will be meat for us this day, Kali.'

He moved on, holding the bearskin close around him, heading south, sheltering the baby, holding the memory of his family within him, feeling the ice in his bones.

It had happened at night, days back, weeks back. They were in the cave, a shallow defenceless place above a frozen river. It was a stopping-off point, a night's shelter in the endless journey south. They were all in there, his mother, his father, his brothers, his sisters, crouched together against the wall. They had a meagre fire, built from logs he'd helped his father to wrench out of the ice. Lak leaned against his mother, stared at the entrance. His father snored, pale moonlight trickled in. His brothers and sisters slept silent, innocent.

'What is the bitterness he holds for me?' he whispered.

'Hush,' his mother whispered.

'What is it?' he whispered. 'As I pulled the timber out I saw such anger gleaming in his eye. And when I stumbled as I carried it he hit me. He took my throat. There was the glare of a beast in him. I saw it again when I sparked the flint, again as the first flames flickered.'

She stroked his brow. 'Hush,' she whispered.

'What is it?'

'He was once like you, but the perils of our world have changed him. He sees in you the strength that was once in him. The strength that in him is fading.'

Lak watched his father in the flickering light.

'And where is the love he held me?' he whispered.

'Hush, my son. Leave these thoughts alone. There will come a time when you alone must be our strength and guide. Prepare yourself for it.' She stroked his brow. 'Lean on me, my son. Sleep. I will watch the entrance.'

And Lak slept, and dreamed of his grandfather, of the old man's tales of the time when the sun shone warm, and green grass and trees filled the valleys.

The snarling woke him, then the sound of his mother's screams . . .

I stopped writing and watched the falling snow. I ran my fingers across the fossilised black tree on my desk. I went downstairs to find Grandpa. He was in the living room, in front of the television. Mum stood in the doorway with her arms folded, watching him. She put her finger to her lips. He was fast asleep. I sat on the sofa beside him. He snored gently, evenly. His eyes flickered beneath his eyelids. There was rubbish on the telly, some game show where they had to answer questions to stop a bucket of black gunge from falling on them. I grinned. There'd be much more interesting things going on behind Grandpa's closed eyes.

I waited for him to wake.

He woke slowly, ever so slowly. Even when his eyes were open his dream continued. He continued to see it, even as his eyes looked towards the nonsense on the telly.

'Kit,' he murmured at last. 'Kit, lad.' His eyes softened, he smiled at me. 'Rubbish, eh?'

'Aye, rubbish.' I switched it off.

'Not out in the snow today, son?'

I shook my head. 'I need to know about John Askew's family,' I said.

'The Askews?' Grandpa rubbed his eyes, pondered. 'Wait till I get it straight. Everything's such a clutter in me head these days. The Askews, aye. I see them now. The grandfather was a good'n. Tough as old boots and a mouthful of curses and too much of a taste for the drink. But gentle enough beneath. Spent many a shift at his side, got to know his ways. He was a man that scared many around him, specially the new lads, but the true nature of him came out when the roof collapsed in 1948. Askew was the man that burrowed through till his hands was bleeding. It was him that carried out the lad that lay in there. Him that saved the lad's life. The father? He's just one of them that's been wasted, son. No proper work for him to do, nothing to control him. Wild as a lad, got wilder as a man. A fighting man. Spent six months in Durham Jail for thumping a lad half to death outside The Fox one night. Afterwards, just took to the drink. Takes it out on his own boy now, and I suspect on his wife. He's a bitter soul, Kit. In another world he might have been fine, but in this one . . .' He shrugged. 'Ah, well. And I hear the boy's heading the same way, too, eh?'

'Could be,' I said.

'Thing is, he's never had a proper childhood, not with that for a father. The baby inside him never had a chance to grow. You understand?'

I nodded. 'I think so.'

Grandpa smiled. 'Maybe the baby's inside him still, still waiting for its chance to show itself and grow.'

I thought of Askew, of the fear and revulsion he caused around him. I recalled the desperation that could be felt within his violent grip, the yearning that could be seen in his violent eyes. Such a strange boy, such a strange mixture of darkness and light. Where *was* the baby in him? And I thought of Lak, whose baby was so obvious, held inside the bearskin.

'Everybody's got the seam of goodness in them, Kit,' said

Grandpa. 'Just a matter of whether it can be found and brought out into the light.'

Eleven

Allie was evil. There was ice in her eye. She'd been enticed, cast under a spell. All the goodness was frozen in her.

She tiptoed towards me with her hands raised like claws.

'Here's evil come for good Kit,' she hissed. 'Here's icy cold and frost to freeze his heart. Here's bitter winds to freeze his soul. Touch my finger, feel the frost there. Touch my cheek, feel the snow there. Look into my eye, see the ice there.'

She came closer, closer, the evil smile grew on her face.

Then she giggled. She danced on the frozen snow. She kicked a storm of white around her.

'Jeez, Kit,' she said. 'It's great! I love it! I just love it!'

We laughed and walked on.

She'd been rehearsing all afternoon. They were putting on Burning Bush's version of *The Snow Queen*. The day it started, Burning Bush had looked around the class with a smile on her face.

'Now, then,' she said. 'I wonder if I can find what I'm looking for. What I need is somebody that can be really really evil. Somebody that can look in your eye and send a chill into your heart. Somebody that can be really good, but that can turn suddenly and be really bad.'

She looked and looked and grinned and grinned.

'Who could it be?' she whispered.

And everybody laughed.

'Allie Keenan!'

Burning Bush smiled. 'Allie Keenan. Of course. Who else.'

Allie giggled again.

'It was great when she picked me. And doing it, it's just . . . Jeez, Kit, man!'

'And guess what,' she said. 'Guess who looked into the hall and smiled, and even winked at me. Dobbs! Terminal Moraine Tectonic Dobbs!' And she danced again. 'I'll be a star!' she said. 'I will! I will! I'll be a star!'

Then she skidded and slipped flat on her back with a thump and she laughed some more.

'It's great,' I said. 'You'll be fantastic.'

'Thank you, Mr Watson. Perhaps you'd like to be my agent.'

I pulled her up and we walked on.

'How's Grandpa?' she said.

'Seems OK now. But it'll come again. No stopping it.'

She clicked her tongue. 'Give him my love.' Then she grunted. 'Ugh. Look. Just look at him.'

It was Askew's father, leaning at the fence. He rolled his head and stared at us. His eyes were red-rimmed, his mouth hung open in a drunken grin.

‘Here they are,’ he slurred. ‘Here they are. Ha!’

We crossed over, so we wouldn’t have to pass close to him.

He swung his arm out with a flourish.

‘Make way! Let them pass!’

He tottered, gripped the fence again. He let out a string of curses.

‘What you looking at?’ he shouted. ‘Eh? Eh? What you looking at?’

‘Brute,’ whispered Allie. ‘Pig.’

‘Come on,’ I said. ‘Hurry up.’

He lurched across the ice on the lane, stood and staggered in our way.

‘Where is he?’ he slurred. ‘Where’s that stupid son of mine?’

We stood there.

‘Eh? Eh? Where is he?’

‘Jeez, Kit,’ said Allie. ‘Come on.’

We walked forward, stood a few feet away from him.

‘Get out the way,’ she said.

‘Aha! Madam says get out the way.’

I gripped the ammonite in my fist.

‘Yes,’ she said. ‘Get out the way, you slob.’

His jaw hung loose. He snarled. He wiped his lips. ‘I said, Where is he?’

‘Gone for good if he’s got any sense,’ said Allie. ‘And I said, Get out the way.’

He took a deep breath. We stepped back as he came closer. He slipped, caught his balance, glared.

'I'll . . . I'll . . .'

We crossed the lane again, hurried on.

'I will,' he said. 'I will. What you looking at?'

We looked back, saw him tottering, waving his fist.

'Look at him,' she said. 'Jeez, Kit. Just look at him.'

I shook my head. 'You're really brave,' I said.

She shivered. 'It was just an act, Kit.'

Twelve

The snarling woke him, then the sound of his mother's screams. Lak gripped the stone axe in his fist. He saw the huge silhouette of the bear in the entrance to the cave. The dying embers of the fire reflected in its eyes. His brothers and sisters cowered against the inner wall. His mother stood before them, her arms outstretched, protecting them. His father crouched low, a rock in his fist. The bear snarled again. It lurched further in, its great paws raised, the great claws glistening. The cave was filled with the stench of its breath. His father leapt from the shadows, struck the bear's head with his rock. The bear swept him aside and he lay unmoving on the earth. Now Lak sprang forward. He caught the beast between the eyes with his axe. He struck again at the bear's arm as it came towards him. He tried to strike again but the bear threw him back against the wall. The children whimpered and screamed. Lak struck the bear's back. He stretched high and struck its head again. His father stirred, yelled at the beast. He flung the rock and it struck the bear's shoulder. Lak struck again – the arm, the neck, the head again. The bear roared and bellowed as it reached down, knocked Lak's mother aside, grabbed one of his sisters by the deerskin that swaddled her and lifted her and carried her out into the night.

They crouched together, whimpering, terror in their eyes, terror in their hearts.

'My baby!' cried Lak's mother. 'Little Dal! My baby!'

Lak's heart thundered. He entered the hell that all boys enter as they come to age. He gripped the axe.

'Our baby!' cried Lak's mother. 'What will we be without our baby?'

Lak held her for a moment.

'Stay here,' he whispered. 'Wait for me.'

And he hurried out into the night.

Already the bear was far away, across the ice. Lak hurried, moving quietly on his deerskin-clad feet. He followed the bear up on to the rock. It moved upwards, towards the crags. He kept losing it, then seeing its silhouette against the thick-starred sky. He heard the baby's cries. He followed, his brain a storm. How could he conquer this beast? What could he do when he was so small against it, when the baby was so delicate? He followed the bear from crag to crag. Dawn came, frail light trickled from the east. The bear headed downward now, towards another valley of ice. There was a narrow passage between steep rocks. The bear hesitated before it blundered onward through the passage. Lak ran like the wind, up on to the rock above the passage. He overtook the bear, running high above it. It raised its head as he passed. It snarled, then blundered on. Lak waited, squatting low on the rock, the axe tight in his fist. This was where the bear would come out from the passage. He heard its feet, its grunted breath, he heard the baby's cries. He waited. As the bear came out he swung the axe against its skull. He struck again and it reeled. And again. And again. The bear roared and tottered. Lak leapt from the rock and as he leapt he struck again. It tumbled. He struck again. It lay on the rock. The baby lay crying on its silent chest. He lifted her and held her tight.

Thirteen

'Dad! Dad!'

Mum was calling from downstairs. 'Dad! Tea up!'

He wasn't with me.

'Dad!'

I went out of my room, looked down at her.

'Wake him up, Kit, eh?'

I knocked on his door, called softly, 'Grandpa!'

No answer. I opened his door. He wasn't there. Just the impression of his body on the quilt. Snow drifted across the window. I went back out, went down to her.

'He's not there,' I said.

'Dad!' she called. 'Dad!'

We looked in the kitchen, in the living room, found nothing.

'Oh, Kit,' she whispered. 'Where's he gone?'

I went to the front door, peered out through the snow, saw the kids out there, obscure little figures sliding and throwing snowballs.

Mum's hand trembled on my shoulder. 'Kit, where can he have gone?'

'He'll be fine,' I said. 'He can't have gone far.'

We stared at each other.

'Call the doctor,' I said. 'I'll go and find him.'

I pulled my coat on and went out there. I narrowed my eyes against the falling snow. I grabbed a boy as he ran past me giggling.

'You seen my Grandpa?' I said.

'Eh?'

His face glowed with the cold. His eyes were shining with delight.

'Eh? Eh? My Grandpa. You seen my Grandpa?'

A snowball thumped into the back of his head. He screamed and giggled.

'Let me go, Kit! They're coming for me!'

'You seen him?'

'Who? No. Not seen nobody. Get off me! Let me go!'

I shoved him away. He sprinted off with snowballs cascading all around him. The gang raced past me in pursuit.

'Come on, Kit!' one of them yelled. 'Let's get him!'

The snow intensified. I started to run, back and forward across the wilderness, all alone. I ran through knots of children playing. I bumped into snowmen, skidded on slides. I kept calling, 'Grandpa! Grandpa!' I grabbed others as I ran. 'You seen my Grandpa?' I kept asking, but they were lost in themselves and their games. 'Eh?' they said. 'Eh? Eh?' I shoved them all away, ran again. I zigzagged, spiralled, yelled and yelled, and came to a halt, gasped for breath, stared uselessly across the wilderness and saw him at last. He was all alone, with his head bowed forward, snow gathering on his hair and cardigan.

'Grandpa!'

He just stood there as I went towards him, as I dusted the snow off him, as I took my coat off and laid it across him. I took his arm, tried to lead him away. He wouldn't move.

'Come on, Grandpa,' I whispered.

There was nothing in his eyes as he looked at me.

'Come on,' I whispered.

He snarled. 'Gerroff,' he said. His voice was harsh, thick, nothing like Grandpa.

I tugged him gently.

'Gerroff, I said.'

'Grandpa. It's me. It's Kit.'

He yelled, like an animal, or a baby.

'Aaaaaah! Aaaaaaah!' He yanked his arm away, tried to run, tumbled into the snow.

I knelt beside him.

'Get him off me! Help! Help!'

A few children gathered around us. They watched. I heard giggling.

'Tell my mum,' I said. 'Go on. Run and tell her I've found him.'

Grandpa cowered. 'Get him off me!'

'Go on!' I yelled, and at last someone sprinted away.

I held my arms around his shoulders. He squirmed, told me to get off. He started to cry like a child.

'Tell him to leave me alone!'

'Grandpa,' I whispered. 'It's Kit. You'll be all right. We'll be home soon.'

I wiped the tears from his cheeks with my fingers.

'Jeez, Kit.'

It was Allie, kneeling beside me. She glared at the watching children.

'Get lost!' she told them. 'Go on! Go to Hell!'

Together, we tugged him to his feet. He was trembling with cold, whimpering with fright.

Allie stroked his brow. 'It's me,' she said. 'Allie. Fairy Queen. The good bad girl.'

At last we saw Mum running through the snow. She held him with me and Allie.

Grandpa stared at our faces.

'It's us,' Mum whispered.

'Gerroff!' he yelled. 'Get them off me!'

Then the doctor came carrying his bag through the snow. He gave Grandpa an injection that calmed him down. He let us lead him through the snow towards home. A snowball thumped on to his back and there were screams of delight as a gang of kids ran away. At home, Allie and I sat downstairs and heard them moving about above us. Melting snow seeped through my clothes. Bitter cold. Allie hunched forward with her chin resting on her fists and stared at the blank wall. Nothing to say. I thought of Lak moving across his wilderness and I feared for him and for the baby. I tried to stop thinking of this and to think of Grandpa instead, but I couldn't stop the story from telling itself inside my head.

'Look at this,' said Allie at last.

She had a penny in her palm. She passed her other hand across it and the penny disappeared. She passed her hand across again and the penny appeared again.

'Magic,' she said.

'Do it again,' I said.

She did it again.

'I have to do it in the play,' she said. 'The Snow Queen teaches me magic. She shows me how to get rid of little things at first, like this penny. Then she shows me how I can use the magic to get rid of the things that get on my nerves. I get rid of things I don't like, little irritations like cabbage and Maths books. Then I start on living things: a dog that barks too much, a bird that wakes me up in the morning. Then I get more evil and I turn on my brother, who keeps telling me to stop being bad and to be good. I just magic him away. It's only when I start to miss him and to see how cruel I've been that I learn how to make the lost things appear again.'

Allie held the penny in her palm. It disappeared and appeared beneath her hand.

'It's really good,' I said.

Soon Dad came in out of the snow and gave us a grim smile and went upstairs. Then an ambulance with its spinning blue lights pulled up in the lane. They brought Grandpa downstairs with a blanket across his shoulders. His face was grey and his eyes were blank and his feet shuffled. As they took him out, Allie went to him and kissed his cheek.

'Hurry home,' she said.

Dad went off with him in the ambulance. Mum came back in and sat beside us.

'He'll be all right,' I whispered.

'Yes, son.'

'Show Mum your trick,' I said to Allie.

Allie put the penny on her palm.

'Now it's gone,' she said. 'Now it's back again.'

'It's from Allie's play at school,' I said. 'She learns how to make things disappear, then she learns how to find the lost things again.'

'Do it again,' said Mum.

The penny was lost and then found again.

Mum lay back in her chair. She clenched her fists. Tears streamed from her closed eyes.

'Do it again,' she said. 'Do it again. Find it again.'

Fourteen

Lak worked quickly. The sun rose slowly into the eastern sky. A gift like this in these bitter days could not be left behind. There was skin enough here to clothe all his brothers and his sisters. He used his grandfather's axe to skin the bear. He first stripped the skin off the beast's arm and wrapped it fur side in around his baby sister. He made a long incision down the front of the bear's chest, others around its throat and across its shoulders. He edged the skin away, exposed the flesh beneath. He sweated, he was smeared in blood. He made incisions down its legs and its other arm and continued cutting and peeling. As he worked, a dog came to his side. It looked shyly at Lak, then lapped at the blood that oozed from the bear.

'Take what you need,' whispered Lak. 'There is enough in this great beast for all of us.'

He worked all morning, until the sun had reached its meagre limit. The baby cried, and Lak dipped his finger into a wound, then gently pressed the finger into her mouth, and the blood dissolved and brought her some nourishment.

'Soon you will be with our mother again,' he told her. 'There will be milk for you again.'

He hurried. He cut away the final stretches of skin. He heaved the naked bloody bear aside. Only its head and paws bore fur now. Lak bowed his head and paid homage to the spirit of the bear. He gave thanks to the gods for the cunning and strength that had caused him to defeat such an adversary. He prayed to his dead grandfather and gave thanks for the gift of the axe that had been handed down through the generations. He looked towards the sun and said the prayer that all of his people prayed now, that the God of the Sun would look kindly upon the people of the ice, that he would come closer to them, that he would fill the air with warmth, would melt the ice and make the valleys green as they had been in ancient days. Then he cut away a piece of the bear's forearm and chewed it. He cut away another piece, and another. Bear was sour meat, but it would give him the strength needed for the return to his family. He gave more fingers of blood to the baby. Then he folded the great skin, hung it across his shoulders, lifted his sister into his arms and headed back towards his family. The dog followed, close behind. Already the sun was sinking, the day was ending.

Lak retraced his path: through the rock passage, across the crags. He moved slowly down towards the great valley of ice. All around, the air continued darkening. The sky began to sparkle with the first stars. Ice began to form on his hair. He held the baby close, he whispered comforts to her.

'Ayeeee! Ayeeee!' he called, wanting to call out the family from the cave.

'Ayeee! Ayeee!' he called out in his exhaustion and triumph.

'Ayeee!' he cried. 'Come out! See Lak again! See our sister Dal brought home safe again!'

No one appeared.

Lak gripped his axe. He crept into the shallow cave. No one. Footprints and the outlines of bodies in the dust. The ashes of a fire. Then he saw against the wall some sticks and a flint. He knelt down and sparked a little fire to life. By its light he saw a little pile of berries and a tiny bird's egg. He squeezed the berries, trickled their juice into Dal's mouth. He sucked the egg from the shell as he had seen his mother do. He mixed it between his teeth. Then he dribbled the mixture from his own mouth to the baby's. He wrapped her close in the bear skin and held her to him. He covered both of them with the rest of the skin. He lay close by the fire. Outside, the darkness deepened, the stars intensified. Tears ran from his eyes. He looked up and saw the charcoal drawing on the cave's wall: a family of stick figures heading south towards the sun. Lak held his sister tight. He felt the dog snuggling against the bear skin. He tried to pray for strength but he was overwhelmed by sleep. He knew that they had been given up as dead.

Fifteen

Allie picked up a pebble, brushed the snow off it, put her evil face on and did her trick. She laughed.

'Just as well you're not playing my brother, Mr Watson, or I'd have to practise getting rid of you.'

We walked on, as far as the river, then we turned right and headed in the direction of Bill Quay.

'Burning Bush says it was the start of magic,' she said. 'A simple trick: you make something disappear, then you make it appear again. Even the cave men did it. The first magicians. They used pebbles and stones like this. They made the people sitting round the fire think that they could send things out of the world and bring them back again.'

I nodded. She put up with my silence. She knew I was preoccupied by Grandpa, but my head was also filled now with storytellers and magicians in dark caves.

'People were scared stiff of them,' said Allie. 'But they honoured them as well. They believed that their magic was a way to conquer death. "Bring the spirit of my mother back," they'd say. "Bring my husband back. Bring my child back."

They gave gifts to the magicians. They even gave them special caves. And the magicians developed bigger tricks, better tricks, and they made the people believe in them and fear them even more.'

The water slopped below us. The ice had reached further from the fringes. Back in Stoneygate, the lights of Christmas trees burned in the windows. A haze hung over the wilderness, icy and sparkling, with children rushing through it. I squinted and saw just ordinary children, children from now.

We passed the place where Askew's den had been. There was just a heap of icy earth that the bulldozer had shoved across it.

'Some day in the far future they'll open up the den,' I said. 'They'll make up stories about what happened in there, just like we make up stories about what happened in the past.'

We walked on.

'Any news?' said Allie.

'Nothing. A couple of days back they said he'd be home for Christmas. Then another day they said he'll never get home again. Who knows?'

She squeezed my arm. 'Jeez,' she whispered. 'All that life in him. All that brilliance, Kit.'

'It's like the world in winter,' I said. 'Like somebody's made everything disappear, and it'll never come back. Like there'll never be enough heat or light again, like nothing'll ever grow again. But it does, like magic.'

She shuddered.

'Brr. Hope it does, Kit. This icy winter's fun, but won't be long till I've had enough of it.'

She put up her hands like claws. She hissed and put her evil face and her evil voice on.

'This is the season of the ice girl. This is the season of evil. This is the season when ice is in the eye and snow is in the heart and frost is in the soul. Protect your soul, for here comes the ice girl.'

'The season of evil,' I echoed. 'Protect your soul.'

'You believe in it?' she asked. 'That there's evil in the world? That it can pursue you and trap you? That we need to be protected?'

'Yes, we need to be protected. There's light and joy, but there's also darkness all around and we can be lost in it.'

'You're making me shiver. Jeez, Kit.' Then she flinched. 'What's that?' she hissed.

'What?'

'What's that in the haze beside the river?'

'Where?' I whispered.

'There, Kit. There!'

And we saw them, the skinny children, and we saw the single child from today among them, making his way through the haze towards us.

'Him,' I hissed.

'Jeez,' she whispered. 'Here comes true evil. Bobby Carr.'

He came out from the haze. He stopped before.

'Askew's gone, you know,' he said. His eyes were wide, excited.

Allie turned her face away.

'Some say he's taken his life,' said Bobby. 'That's what the game was all heading for. In the end he'd take his own life, and it wouldn't be a game.'

'Rubbish,' whispered Allie.

'They say he'll be found in the river. They say that Jax has ripped him limb from limb.'

He moved closer, spoke quieter.

'They say his dad's done it, that he's done what he's threatened to do, and killed his own son.'

'You moron,' said Allie.

'Kit doesn't think so,' said Bobby. 'Do you, Kit?'

'You're a disease,' said Allie.

'He wouldn't,' I said. 'And his dad wouldn't. And if I were you I'd stop spreading stupid tales.'

Bobby grinned. 'Tales!' he said. 'But I bet you can't walk by the river now without looking to see if Askew's body's floating there. And I bet you know that Askew's dad could do anything if he was drunk enough.'

He sneered at Allie.

'You,' he said. 'You don't know nothing. You're just an airhead. That's what Askew said.'

She raised her claws and stepped towards him and he sprinted away.

'Disease,' she hissed. She shook her head. 'If Askew's got any sense he'll just have got himself away from this stupid place.'

We walked on in silence, kept turning our eyes to the water, hoping to see nothing there. Behind us, skinny children whispered in fright.

Sixteen

I began to dream. I began to blend with Lak. I crouched in the cave, by the fire. The bearskin on my back was heavy. I felt the bear's dried, decaying blood against my skin. My throat and nostrils were filled with the reek and sting of smoke. The walls were covered with great beasts, tiny humans moving in fear around them and flickering in the firelight. The magician wore a string of teeth around his throat. Blue tattooed gashes streaked his face. A bear was painted in red upon his chest. He carried a skull in one hand, a thigh bone in the other. He glistened with sweat. Somewhere someone thumped a drum, and he raised each foot in turn and stamped it on the earth. He grunted, whimpered, groaned. The people around the fire trembled in fear of him but held out their hands to him. Lak's mother was at my side. She held a clutch of shining coloured stones in her filthy palm.

'Bring my son back,' she asked. 'Bring my baby back.'

The magician rocked and his eyes swivelled. He crouched, and swept his bare hands slowly through the flames. A dish of berries appeared in his hand. We picked the berries as he handed them to us and we ate them, hard bitter juiceless things that caught in our throats as we swallowed them. The magician danced again.

'Bring my son back,' said Lak's mother. 'Bring my baby back.'

My head rocked and my senses reeled. The magician threw dust into the fire and it flickered, flared, pink smoke filled the cavern. We stood up and danced with the magician around the fire. I held the ammonite out to him.

'Bring my Grandpa back,' I said.

Lak's mother tugged my arm. I met her eye.

'Bring my son back,' she said. 'You. Bring my baby back.' She pressed the shining stones into my hand. 'Bring them back to me,' she said.

I tugged away from her, and then I knew no more until I opened my eyes to the white light of my room, snow falling yet again, Mum calling,

'Kit! Come on! Allie will be here soon!'

I held the ammonite in my fist. Beneath it in my skin were the impressions left by Lak's mother's tiny coloured stones.

Seventeen

Midwinter. The dark days of December. Short bright days, long dark nights. The Christmas lights intensified. Pyramids of lights on Christmas trees. Strings of coloured lights that flashed, flickered, danced, chased each other around the edges of the windows. They hung in naked garden trees beneath the stars that shone and trembled in the endless sky. Snow stopped falling but the bitter cold remained. The snow on the wilderness turned hard as stone. Our footprints and our snowballs lay out there like white fossils. Snowmen stood like ancient statues. On the river, the ice continued to inch out from the edges. Carols drifted through the air from radios and hi-fis. We practised them at school: *Good King Wenceslas*, *Silent Night*, *The Holly and the Ivy*. In the evenings, children moved through Stoneygate in little groups, and sang in our gardens.

In the deep midwinter, frosty wind made moan,
Earth stood hard as iron, water like a stone.
Snow had fallen snow on snow, snow on snow,
In the deep midwinter, long ago . . .

At home, we turned the heating higher and higher. We prayed that Grandpa would be well again. Inside ourselves, we prayed that if he was to die, then he shouldn't be made to bear great pain or a deepening of his confusion. When we visited him in hospital we found him frail and small. Sometimes he knew us and he whispered our names and touched our faces with trembling fingers. At other times he stared past us through empty eyes into the immense absence that surrounded him.

We returned home in silence to Stoneygate and sat beside our Christmas tree and whispered stories of the man he had been. I lay at night with my head close to the wall, remembering him beside me as he arranged his souvenirs and sang of being in his prime. I clutched the ammonite, I ran my fingers across the fossil tree. I wrote of the pit children playing at dusk beside the river. I gazed out there, squinted, saw them there, little skinny things at liberty in the wilderness. I stopped squinting, they disappeared. I wrote my story about Lak and his wilderness, and sought a way to bring Lak and his sister home. I read about the great convulsions of the earth, of the continents shifting away from each other, colliding with each other. I wrote of ice that was powerful enough to move mountains. I wrote of ancient seas whose sediment lay a hundred feet and a hundred million years beneath Stoneygate. I dreamed of Silky, who led me through endless tunnels before leaving me alone in the dark. I dreamed of magicians who danced in darkness, storytellers who whispered through flames. I felt the hand of Lak's mother gripping mine, felt brightly-coloured pebbles in my palm. In the deepest night I heard a frail voice singing – *When I was young and in me pri-ime* – but I woke to find it was nothing but illusion.

Allie was engulfed by *The Snow Queen.* She sparkled with the joy of it, so intensely that it seemed there truly was ice and frost in her eyes. She practised before me, raised her claws, hissed her lines, prowled delicately and dangerously across the snow, exploded into laughter and kicked a storm of frozen snow around us. Burning Bush told me how brilliant Allie was, what a natural she was. She was right to set her dreams on acting. She winked. We'd have to watch it didn't go too much to her head. As the first performance approached, Allie's change into the ice girl quickened. She switched instantly from being who she was in life to who she was in the play.

'Who's me?' she asked one day as we walked home from school. 'Who's Allie Keenan? This almost-nice one, or this truly-bad one?' She laughed. 'That's why I love it, Kit. It's like magic. I don't just have to be me. The world doesn't just have to be the way it is. You can change it, and keep on changing it.'

I nodded. I knew that from my stories and my dreams.

Eighteen

There was no sign of John Askew. Posters were stuck to walls and telegraph poles. They asked: HAVE YOU SEEN THIS BOY? They carried a photograph of his face, a description of his clothes – black jeans and coat and hat, T-shirt with *Megadeth* upon it – of his black dog Jax. Policemen searched the wilderness and the banks of the river. They spread wide, opened the abandoned sheds and warehouses downstream. They peered into little kid's dens. They floated in little boats on the river, peered down into the murk, reached beneath the ice below the banks. They walked into the hills beyond Stoneygate, carrying maps of old mines and pitshafts. There was much rumouring and whispering: he'd slipped on the ice, tumbled into the bitter river, he'd been drowned and washed towards the sea. He'd thrown himself in there, he'd been driven to it by an evil drunken father. Or he'd fallen into an ancient pitshaft, or the dog had turned on him and killed him, or he'd be found frozen in the deep snow when the thaw came. The worst tale was whispered behind cupped hands, spoken in quiet corners: it was the father himself who'd done his son to death.

One day the police took Askew's father away, and Stoneygate was filled with the story that the body had been found, that murder had been done, that the father had at last been arrested. But there was no truth in the tale. The father was brought back home, and that night I heard him calling through my dreams. I got up, went to my window and saw him at the fence. He stood there with his arms outstretched. He howled into the empty wilderness:

'Johnny Askew! Johnny Askew! Oh, come back home!'

I passed near the Askew house with Allie one bitter afternoon. Closed curtains. No Christmas lights. The mother came to the door as we stood there. She had the baby in her arms.

'What you two looking at?' she yelled.

'Come on, Kit,' whispered Allie.

'Come to get your eyeful?' she yelled.

'Kit,' whispered Allie.

'You! You and your kind! Why can't you bloody well leave us alone?'

Allie tugged me.

'Just a minute,' I said.

I went into the cul-de-sac, towards Askew's garden.

The woman glared as I approached. I saw the baby's thick dark hair, her broad face, saw how her brother's features were held in hers in gentler form. She cried and squirmed in her mother's arms. I stood before the low wicker fence.

'There's no news yet?' I said.

The woman scowled at me. 'News! What's news to the likes of you? Nowt but bad news you're after. Nowt but doom and death'll satisfy you.'

The baby bawled.

'I was John's friend,' I said.

She watched me, suspicious.

'I was. I talked to him. He gave me one of his drawings.'

'You!' she said.

'Yes,' I said. 'But there's no news?'

'Nowt.'

'I think he'll be all right,' I said. 'I think he's just run away and he'll come back again.'

She watched me.

'I do,' I said. 'He told me that's what he wanted to do.'

She clicked her tongue.

'Aye,' she said. 'He threatened many times. What's your name?'

'Kit Watson.'

'He mentioned you.' She rested her knuckle on the baby's lips, allowed it to suck. 'She misses him,' she said. 'The big daft brute. She misses him like Hell.' She sighed, then started to glare again. 'You don't know nothing, do you? This isn't some stupid game you're playing with him?'

I shook my head.

'Aye. Well. It'll turn out somehow, there's no doubt.'

Her husband appeared in the doorway behind her. His eyes met mine.

'What's he after?' he said.

She shook her head.

'Concerned for our John, that's all.'

'Come back in,' he said. 'You'll catch your death.'

She started to turn away. 'If you hear anything,' she said. 'Anything at all.'

'Yes,' I said.

Askew's dad stood aside to let her in. His eyes met mine again.

'Heard about your Grandpa,' he said. 'A good man. Not like the rest of the rabble. Give him me best.'

Nineteen

I opened the door a few inches and slipped into the hall. I stood there in the darkness, facing the lighted stage. I thought I'd not be seen, but Burning Bush turned in her chair and saw me there. She narrowed her eyes, pretended to be angry, but she grinned and pressed her finger to her lips. Eerie music played: violins out of tune, squeaky tin whistles. The Snow Queen sat in her white furs on her throne of ice. Behind her, snow-clad mountains filled the world. A pale sun hung low in the pale sky above them. A boy backed towards the Snow Queen from the wings. He was dressed in red and green. He held his trembling hands before his face. The Snow Queen smiled coldly, watched him, as Allie the ice girl entered the stage, calmly following her brother. She was all in silver, her hair was stainless steel, her claws were blades. Her eyes were bitter and her voice was cruel and sharp as ice:

'Here's evil sister come for good kind brother. Here's icy cold and frost to freeze his heart. Here's bitter winds to freeze his soul. Touch this finger, feel the frost there. Touch this cheek, feel the snow there. Look into this eye, see the ice there.'

The boy backed away from her.

'Sister,' he begged. 'Sister. What's happening to you?'

Allie grinned and continued to tiptoe towards him.

The boy bumped into the Snow Queen's throne and fell to the ground in fright.

'Sister,' he said. 'Sister!'

'What shall we do with this creature?' said the Snow Queen.

Allie touched him with the toe of her silver boot.

'What shall we do to such a silly boy?' she said.

'Shall we put ice in his eye also?' said the Queen.

The boy cowered, covered his face. 'Sister,' he said. 'Come back to me.'

Allie laughed. 'He could never be an ice boy,' she said. 'He doesn't have the courage to be an ice boy.'

The Snow Queen reached out and stroked Allie's claws.

'Not like you, my dear,' she said. 'Then tell me, little evil courageous one: what shall we do with him? What shall we do with good kind brother?'

Allie hissed. She sighed. She wondered.

She knelt down and stroked her brother. 'I'm tired of him,' she said.

'Then lose him,' said the Queen.

Allie closed her eyes and smiled, and hissed and sighed again.

'Lose him?'

'Yes,' said the Queen.

'Yes,' Allie whispered. 'Yes.'

'Let us lose him,' said the Queen. 'Let us send him to oblivion. Let us send him to where there is nothing and no one. Let us send him from our sight.'

Allie grinned. 'Yes,' she hissed. 'That is the answer.'

The boy scrambled away from her.

'Now?' said Allie.

The Snow Queen gazed upon her.

'I have taught you what you need to know. Do it now, my clever girl.'

Allie pointed to her brother. 'Be gone!' she called.

And there was a flash of brilliant light, a crack of lightning, and the boy was gone.

'Wonderful!' called Burning Bush. 'Much better, everyone! Now, let's look at scene thirteen again.' She turned in her chair again, pointed at me. 'And you, Christopher Watson,' she called. 'Be gone!'

I laughed, and slipped back into the corridor.

'How d'you do it?' I asked Allie that afternoon.

She grinned. 'With great talent, Mr Watson.'

'No. I mean, how do you make him disappear?'

'Ah. That's secret, I'm afraid. It's magic, that's all you need to know.'

I looked at her.

'And it's magic when I bring him back again,' she said.

'You,' I said.

She grinned again. 'Me what?'

I laughed. 'Nothing.'

Allie danced in the frozen snow. 'Go on,' she said. 'Say it!' She giggled and stamped the frozen snow.

'Say what?' I said.

'Hahaha! Say what? Say I do, don't I? I drive you wild!'

Twenty

Sundays were the worst days to see Grandpa. The sunlight that poured into the ward made his face more pale, his eyes more empty. We sat around him sipping tea. We touched his arm. We called him Grandpa, Dad. We murmured our names to him.

'It's me,' I'd say. 'Grandpa, it's me. It's Kit.'

Sometimes he smiled weakly and seemed about to speak to us, but it was as if he lost all energy, and he didn't know how to break out of his confusion. He simply gazed through us, through the windows, through the world. He worsened as the winter deepened. Deeper silence. Deeper loneliness. It seemed he was lost to us, he'd never get back to us. We left him there, travelled home through the bitter dusk in our own deep bitter silence.

Then that Sunday I pressed the ammonite into his fist. He held it with his fingers.

'Remember?' I whispered. 'You gave it to me, from a million years ago.'

We watched his fingers awkwardly touching the

indentations on the ancient shell, tracing its spirals.

'It comes from the sea,' I said. 'From the coal a hundred feet under Stoneygate.'

He raised his eyes and stared at me, through me.

'You were young,' I said. 'You were in your prime.'

Mum stroked my back. I heard her fingers telling me: *Don't, Kit. Don't make it more difficult for yourself.*

'Remember,' I told him. 'Grandpa. Remember.'

He closed his eyes and touched the ammonite.

'Kit,' Mum said. 'Don't, Kit.'

'Grandpa,' I carried on. 'You told me the world was engulfed by memory. You told me you kept on seeing everything you've ever seen. You told me all my stories. You told me memory was the most precious thing.'

I pressed the ammonite hard into his palm.

'Grandpa. Grandpa.'

He sighed, his fingers loosened, I caught the ammonite as it spilled towards the floor.

Mum put her arm around me, pulled me to her.

'Drink your tea, love,' she whispered.

I sipped the tea. There seemed nothing more to do. Then I tried again. I leaned close to him again.

'Grandpa,' I whispered. 'Listen. Once upon a time there was a boy called Silky. We called him that cos of the way the lamplight fell on him, cos it made him shine like flickering silk as he flashed through the tunnels before our eyes. A glimpse, and then he's gone . . .'

I watched him. Nothing.

'A little lad in shorts and boots that many of us seen down there, sometimes just looking at us from the deepest edges of the dark, sometimes slipping past our backs as we leaned down to the coal. If ever a lamp went out or a pitman's bait was pinched, that's Silky's work, we used to say . . .'

Grandpa's face softened. Something like a smile on him. Then a voice, a murmur, his lips hardly moving. Distant, frail, ancient.

'Little mischief,' I whispered.

His voice echoed the sound and rhythm of my own.

'That's right,' I said.

That smile again, that frail voice again.

'Little Silky,' I whispered.

The echo again.

'Some said he'd been trapped down there after one of the disasters,' I said. 'One they'd never been able to get to. One of those that never got taken out and buried. Not scary, though. Something sweet in him. Something you wanted to touch and comfort and draw out into the light.'

That smile again. He opened his eyes. His eyes met mine for a moment. I saw the depth of wondering in them.

'Little Silky,' I said. 'Ask any of the old blokes round here and they'll tell you about our Silky . . .'

Grandpa hissed the word, 'Silky'.

'That's right,' I whispered. 'Silky. You remember. He took the water and biscuits we left him. Little mischief.'

A tiny laugh, deep inside his throat.

'A thing of brightness,' I said. 'Deep down there in the dark.'

He lifted his hand, trembling, touched my face, gazed into my eyes.

'It's Kit,' I whispered.

He blinked, and looked, and blinked again.

He smiled, ran his tongue across his lips.

He said the word: *Kit*.

Then looked at each of us, then closed his eyes.

We let him sleep.

'Find Silky in your dreams,' I whispered. 'He'll keep you safe until they come through the tunnels with the lamps.'

We sat there looking at each other, didn't dare to speak our hopes. We sipped tea for a while, then went out together into the midwinter night.

Twenty One

Silky came again that night. Just a glimpse, from the corner of my eye. A shimmer in the corner of my room. I closed my eyes, ran after him through endless tunnels, headed deep into the earth. I smiled when our eyes met, when I knew that he was waiting for me, that he was leading me. I smiled as we ran, with nothing to be seen but his flickering before me, nothing to be heard but the thundering of my heart and the gasping of my breath and the thumping of my feet. We ran an age, a million years, until his final flickering and he was gone for good.

I stretched my hands out, tiptoed forward, touched Grandpa.

'Grandpa,' I whispered.

'Kit,' he said.

We held each other tight for hours, until at last we heard the footsteps in the tunnel, saw the distant lights of the lamps, heard the voices of the men who'd come to find us.

'Here they are,' I whispered.

'Here they are,' he said. 'We're okay, son. Here they are.'

Twenty Two

The baby woke him, sobbing against his chest. Light filled the entrance to the cave, the endless ice outside. Lak reached into the bearskin and touched his sister's lips.

'Hush, my sweet,' he whispered.

He stared at his family on the cave wall, heading south. He turned his eyes away, stood up, and went out to the ice. He clawed ice into his palm, let it melt there, dribbled water into the baby's mouth, dribbled water into his own. He squeezed the last of the berries and fed her with them. The dog crouched by him, licking ice. Lak stroked him, whispered comfort to him. He went back into the cave. He cut the bearskin into two pieces with the axe, flung one into the corner of the cave, wrapped the other around himself and the baby. He lifted the flint, gripped his grandfather's axe, stepped out into the valley, didn't turn back.

He headed south.

He climbed away from the ice, onto the crags where he found bitter plants to feed them with. He gave the only sweet part of the plants, the blossom, to the baby. He cast his eyes across the wilderness, seeking a sign. A mammoth lurched across the valley. A pair of tiny deer leapt away across the rock. Tiny skylarks rose, hung over him with their brilliant song. Much higher, huge dark birds circled slowly, biding their time.

Lak called: 'Ayeeee! Ayeeeee!' hoping to hear at last some call that was not just the echo of his own.

As they moved on, the baby whimpered and wept. He whispered to her, caressed her, but felt how she was becoming thin, heard how her voice was already becoming frailer. He found more bitter plants for her. He melted ice in his palms and dribbled it into her mouth. Then they came upon a hollow in the rocks, a patch of scrubby earth where two deer nibbled at the meagre grass. Lak crouched, gripped Kali at his side, held its mouth tight shut. Edged closer, saw that they were male and female. The male lifted its head, pricked its ears, sniffed the air, looked nervously around the crags. Bent its head again, nibbled again. Lak prayed to The Sun God, to the spirits of his ancestors. The baby began to whimper, the deer stirred. Lak stood and flung his axe. It struck the female. She staggered, tried to move away, but then Kali was upon her, his teeth at her throat, then Lak, who ended her life with the crack of a rock at her skull.

Lak raised his arms in triumph. He wiped his hands in the deer's blood. He smeared it across his face. He paid homage to the spirit of the deer, thanked the Sun God and his ancestors. He took the baby out and held her to the deer's udder. He squeezed.

'Suck, my sweet,' he whispered.

He squeezed. She sucked. He saw the milk spilling from the teat, from the edges of his sister's mouth. He saw her swallowing. He licked his lips, tasted the blood there, grinned.

The baby drank hungrily, pressed close against the deer's still-

warm belly. The dog lapped the blood at the deer's skull. He lifted the baby from the teat, laid her in her bearskin in the sunlight. He opened the deer's flesh with the axe and cut strips of meat away. He ate the meat, chewed hungrily, the blood dribbled from his lips. Deer meat, sweeter and tenderer than that of the bear. He threw pieces for the dog. He ate until he felt that his belly would burst. He put the baby to the teat again. He squeezed and she sucked.

'Ayeee!' he called softly. 'Ayeee!'

The sun shining into the hollow became stronger. He lay with the baby and tickled her. She gurgled softly and smiled. He made her drink once more, then he drank himself, sucking at the teat. He shoved strips of meat into his pouch, then lifted his sister and moved on again out of the hollow, back on to the crags above the ice. He moved quickly, with hope in his heart. The baby slept, contented.

Behind them, the great dark birds spiralled from the sky, flapped heavily down into the hollow.

Twenty Three

We were at the kitchen table, with the story.

'Jeez, Kit,' she said. 'How do you do it?'

I laughed. 'Magic.'

She thumped me in the ribs. 'You,' she said.

'Drive you wild, eh?'

'Drive me wild.'

'What'll happen to them next?'

I shrugged. 'Dunno.'

'Dunno? How can you not know?'

'Just how it is. Stories are living things, like Burning Bush says. Might be something terrible waiting for them at the next crag. Might be no more food. The baby might die. Lak might fall off a cliff.'

'Jeez, Kit. I thought you just made them do what you want them to do. Plan it, then write it.'

'Sometimes it's like that. But when the people in them start to live . . . You can't really keep them in control.'

She flicked through the pages of the story.

'I know what I want to happen,' I said. 'I want to keep

them safe and get them to the family again. But . . .'

'But there's bears out there, and vultures. All kinds of dangers.'

'Yes. Yes.'

'Poor souls. Still, I suppose it's just a story in the end.'

I shrugged.

'Yes, I suppose so.' I laughed. 'But Lak's mother comes to me at night.'

'Lak's mother what?'

'She comes to me at night. She tries to give me gifts. She tells me to bring her son and her baby home.'

'Jeez, Kit.'

'It's really like she's really there,' I said.

'Brilliant,' she said. 'Dead scary.'

'See?' I said.

'See what?'

'Magic. Telling stories is a kind of magic.'

'You've not shown Burning Bush yet.'

'No. When it's done. Anyway, it's not just for her. It's for John Askew.'

'Him?'

'Yes, him. I told I'd write a story and he could do the illustrations for it.'

'If he comes back again. If the worst hasn't happened.'

'Yes, if he comes back again and the worst hasn't happened.'

'Let's hope,' she said.

'That's another part of the magic,' I said.

'What is?'

'I think if Lak and his sister's safe, then Askew'll be safe. And if he's safe, they'll be safe.'

She stared at me. 'Jeez, Kit. What d'you mean?'

'I'm not sure,' I said. 'But I'm sure it's true.'

Twenty Four

'Poor lost soul,' said Mum.

We looked out. There she was, Askew's mother, with the baby in her arms, walking aimlessly through the frozen wilderness.

'Poor soul,' she said again. 'You'd not do anything like that to us?'

I shook my head. 'No.'

'I know. But there's still the fear, whatever you know. Come on, eh? Let's go.'

It was Sunday afternoon. A visit to Grandpa again. We got into the car, headed out of Stoneygate. I carried Askew's picture rolled up in my hand. I carried the ammonite in my pocket. I carried all the stories in my head.

We sat down in a little group around him. We drank tea. He stared at us and through us. But he sat straight, his hands didn't tremble, there was light in his eyes.

'Dad?' said Mum.

He blinked, refocused, smiled at her, at each of us in turn.

He touched my dad's arm. 'Hello, son,' he whispered, so frail.

I saw the tears in Dad's eyes as he held him.

Grandpa touched each of us, whispered each of our names. He lifted his tea with skinny cupped hands, sank back in his chair.

'All wore out,' he whispered.

He laughed, a little weak noise in the back of his throat. He winked, slowly, unsteadily, laughed again.

'Been off with the fairies again, eh?' he said.

'A long way off,' said Mum.

'Ah, well.' He drank again.

'I brought this for you, Grandpa,' I said.

I unrolled the drawing, held it before him.

'Well, I never.'

His eyes searched the drawing's darkness.

'Little Silky,' he whispered. 'Just as he was.'

'It's for you, Grandpa. They can hang it by your bed for you.'

'Nice. Nice.' He smiled, lost in the drawing. 'Little mischief,' he whispered.

Then leaned forward, put his fingers to his lips.

'Comes to me at night, you know,' he said. 'Comes and sees me in me dreams. Comes to keep me safe.' He winked, raised his finger. 'Don't tell this lot here, mind. They'll think I'm crackers.'

We laughed, with tears in our eyes.

He fell asleep. We watched his eyes shifting and flickering

beneath their lids. I imagined Silky in there with him, keeping him safe. Dad talked to one of the doctors. Yes, it might be possible for him to come home for Christmas. We sat and watched him as the darkness deepened outside. I put the rolled-up picture in his lap.

When we left, he was singing in his sleep.

When I was young and in me pri-ime . . .

At home, Askew's mother passed us, coming off the wilderness.

Mum touched her shoulder, held her arm. 'He'll be all right,' she said. 'I'm sure John'll be all right.'

Mrs Askew lowered her head. The baby's face shone from within the thick warm coverings that held her.

'Come in and have some tea,' said Mum.

She shook her head.

'Not now,' she said. 'Get this one home into her bed.' She looked at our faces She reached out and gripped my hand.

'Bring him home,' she whispered. 'Bring my boy home.' Her fingernails and her rings dug into my skin. 'Bring him home.'

Then she hurried homeward through the dark.

Twenty Five

The Snow Queen night. The moon shed its light on to the wilderness as we walked to school. It stunned the light from stars. It made snow luminous. It glittered in our eyes. It cast shadows into the gardens of Stoneygate, into the ruts and depressions of the frozen earth. Our own shadows moved silently at our side. We held our collars tight and sent plumes of silvery breath into the air. There were dozens of us, families coming out from Stoneygate to watch the Snow Queen slide a sliver of ice into Allie's eye and sow evil in her soul. Young children giggled in excitement, clasped the hands of parents. Old people walked tentatively, took careful steps, used rubber-tipped sticks to keep them safe. Beyond its fence, the school gleamed with warm electric light.

Inside the doorway, first years dressed in silver foil and silver slippers passed out programmes. We read that this was not a suitable play for young children on their own. The lobby had great paintings and photographs of glaciers and ice floes. There were paintings of polar bears and penguins. The humps of whales burst from clearings in the ice. Maps showed how the Ice Ages once held the northern world in its grip. Fur-clad people hunched in caves around blazing fires beneath paintings of the beasts they feared, hunted and worshipped. Music played: squeaky violins and whistles, sometimes a distant wailing voice, sometimes a roaring beast.

Chambers stood there, directing us inward. He smiled, shook my parents' hands, told them I seemed to have pulled myself together after the troubles with the game. Dobbs winked at me, shook my parents' hands as well, whispered that the school had great hopes for me. We filed into the hall: dim lights inside, rows of chairs facing the brilliantly-lit ice world on the stage. Then all the lights went down, left us all in deepest darkness. A gasp of mock-fright from the children, then *The Snow Queen* began.

Two children who'd taken a wrong turning, became lost in this world of ice. They wore red and green, they held hands, they looked around in fascination and fear. They talked of the home they'd lost, their loving parents, the green hills and valleys around it. How had they gone so wrong? The boy wept and the girl comforted him, then scoffed him for his weakness, his lack of courage. She pointed across the mountains: It's that way, she told him. She was sure it was that way. The boy whimpered. How could she know that? How could she know? They quarrelled. She threatened to leave him on his own. She grinned down at him. *Look at you*, she whispered. *Just look at you*. Then the Snow Queen came to the edge of the stage in her sleigh and the look that passed between her and Allie sent a shiver down my spine.

She stepped down from the sleigh and wrapped the children in her arms. She cooed at them, comforted them. She told them that there was no need for fear. She wrapped them in white furs. She stroked their cheeks, their hair. *Such pretty children*, she whispered.

'Children often take the wrong move,' she said. 'They go wandering in winter. They seek the deeper snow, for their snowmen, for their games. They take the wrong path. They become lost souls. They find themselves in my kingdom.'

The boy whimpered, looked down, chewed his trembling lips. 'Who are you?' Allie whispered.

'I am the Snow Queen. I rule the ice and snow and bitter winds. I am the queen of frozen hearts. Touch my cheek, feel the ice there.'

Allie reached out, touched the Snow Queen's perfect white skin.

'You're beautiful,' she whispered.

'Touch my lips, feel the frost there.'

Allie touched and sighed.

'My brother's so scared,' she said. 'He wants so much to be home again.'

They looked at the silent trembling boy.

'No need for fear,' said the queen. 'You understand that, don't you?'

'Yes,' said Allie.

'Look into my eyes. See the endless winter there.'

'Yes,' said Allie.

The Snow Queen smiled.

'So pretty,' she whispered. 'Such clear clever eyes.'

She wrapped Allie in her arms, led her away from the boy.

'Many children come,' she said. 'They shiver, whimper, whine and cry. They want green valleys, cosy villages, little homes with fires burning.' She fondled Allie's cheek. 'I dream of a winter child, a child who wants to stay with me.'

She reached down, lifted a jagged piece of ice, held it before Allie's face. 'See how beautiful it is?' she whispered.

'Yes.'

'Let me rest it on your cheek. Feel its perfect bitter cold.'

'Bitter perfect cold,' said Allie.

The Snow Queen snapped a tiny fragment from the ice.

'Turn your eyes to me, my child.'

Allie turned her eyes. The music squeaked and wailed. The Snow Queen gently slid the ice into Allie's eye.

And Allie's evil started. She learned the magic: how to make small things disappear, then larger things. Her evil grew. She became bored by her brother. She pointed her finger at him and sent him from the world.

During the interval Mum went on about how wonderful Allie was, how terrifying. Beyond her, through the knots of adults drinking tea, I saw Bobby Carr. He leaned in a doorway, watched me, smiled softly. He winked, beckoned me with a backward movement of his head. I turned away. He was a disease, like Allie said. He kept on watching, smiling. I made my way through the people towards him.

'What?' I whispered.

He raised his eyes and grinned, then stared at me. 'You're dead,' he said.

'Eh?'

'Askew's back. You're dead.'

'Where is he?'

'Somewhere. And he's asking about you.'

'What d'you mean?'

'Asking. About. You.' He smiled. 'And. You're. Dead.'

I grabbed him by the arm and dragged him out into the corridor. I shoved him against the wall, against a painting of an ancient valley of ice.

'You're a disease,' I said. 'Where is he?'

'Somewhere.'

I shoved him hard against the wall.

'He's come back full of Hell,' said Bobby. 'And he wants to see you.'

He took out a drawing from his pocket, unfolded it.

'He gave me this for you.'

I turned it up to the light. It showed both of us, Askew and me. We were in a cave. We were almost naked. We had knives in our fists and we faced each other across a blazing fire. The names of the dead were scratched into the walls. From the edges of the dark, dozens of skinny children watched.

'If you tell, he'll kill us both,' Bobby whispered.

'Kill!' I said. 'Ha!'

'Yes, kill. Him and Jax. Tell nobody.'

'You worm,' I whispered.

Then I saw Chambers watching us from the far, dimly-lit end of the corridor.

'Tell nobody,' Bobby said again, then he hurried towards the lobby and the night.

'All right now, Christopher?' said Chambers, coming towards me.

I shoved the drawing into my pocket.

'Yes, sir.'

We heard Burning Bush calling that the second half was about to start.

'It's scary stuff, eh?' said Chambers.

'Yes, sir.'

He contemplated me. 'It's very strange, Christopher. This desire we have to be scared, to be terrified, to look into the darkness.'

'Yes, sir.'

He looked along the corridor through which Bobby had disappeared.

'It can of course lead us astray, Christopher.' He looked into my eyes again. 'As you know very well yourself, eh?'

'Yes, sir.'

He smiled. 'Keep the darkness on the stage, eh? Keep it in books. They're the places for it, eh?'

'Yes, sir.' He touched my shoulder.

'Come on, Christopher. Time for Alison to terrify us again.'

We pushed through the door. I saw Mum searching the crowds for me, fear beginning to haunt her eyes.

The play began again, but I was lost in my own thoughts, my own fears. I felt the sweat on my palms and the quickened beat of my heart. I knew that Askew would call me soon, that he would choose the time and place. And I knew that eventually I would go into the darkness with him, that it would be my task to bring him home.

Twenty Six

Past midnight. Couldn't sleep. Sat at my desk, tried to write Lak's tale, tried to get him across the crags, to find the warm cave of his lost family. I couldn't write it. I stared out into the wilderness. I squinted, saw the shapes of skinny children playing by the river in the moonlight. Stopped squinting, the skinny children disappeared. Looked up at the three drawings: me; Silky; me and Askew in the cave. Whispered my Grandpa's song: *When I was young and in me pri-ime . . .* Fingered the ammonite, the pony, the fossil bark. Closed my eyes, saw Silky flickering at the corners of my mind. Prayed for Grandpa. Smelt woodsmoke, bodies, sweat, opened my eyes again, saw her, Lak's mother. She crouched in the corner of my room in her animal skins. She held out the coloured pebbles to me. Her mouth opened, closed, silently formed the words: *Bring my son back. Bring my baby back.* I looked away, looked back, she didn't disappear. Looked out, saw the dark hunched shape, the black dog. Askew.

I watched. He didn't disappear. I pulled my clothes on,

tiptoed out into the night. No sign of him. I hurried across the crackling snow towards the river.

'Askew,' I whispered. 'Askew!'

No answer. I looked around me. Nothing. Pulled my jacket close.

'Askew!'

Across the wilderness, the one light in our street was the reading lamp on my desk, shining down on the tale of Lak, illuminating the hunched form of his mother crouching against the wall. I shivered.

'Who's this?' I heard.

'Who's there?' I said. 'Askew?'

There were little whispers, little giggles, little thin voices.

'Who's this? Who's this? Who's this?'

There were children all around. I saw them at the corner of my eye. They peered at me. They were skinny, half-naked. Pale bodies, great staring eyes in blackened faces.

'Who's this?' they whispered to each other. 'Who's this?'

They giggled.

'Kit Watson,' they whispered. 'Christopher Watson, aged thirteen.'

I turned and turned, trying to see them true, but then Askew spoke, and there was silence, just Jax's growls.

'Down, boy!'

His voice had deepened. His face had darkened. His shoulders were broader. He wore heavy layers of dark clothes. His head hung forward, his hair was filthy and wild.

'Askew.'

'Mr Watson.'

'Where you been, Askew?'

'Away.'

'Your mother's ill with worry. Your baby sister . . .'

'And him?'

'Him, too,' I said. 'He wants you home again.'

'Ha!'

I trembled. I saw the tiny faces, peeping over at us from the river's edge, heard the thin breath again, the fearful whispers.

'I've come for you, Kit.'

'Me?'

'You. You're the only one.'

I stared, pulled my coat close again.

'You see them,' he whispered. 'Don't you, Kit?'

The eyes above the frozen snow, watching, goggling. The hiss of their breath, their whispers.

'You do,' he said. Jax growled.

'Yes,' I whispered.

'And you see other things. Things that don't exist for other eyes.'

'Yes,' I whispered.

He stepped towards me. 'This is because you're dead, Kit. You see through the eyes of the dead. Here you are, among the dead.'

'Askew, man. That's stupid.'

A murmur from the children.

'Kit Watson,' they whispered. 'Christopher Watson, aged thirteen.'

Askew laughed. 'Remember, Kit. John Askew, aged thirteen. Christopher Watson, aged thirteen. Written in stone beneath the trees. It waited for you.'

'It was long ago, Askew.'

'Things from long ago keep coming back and coming back. The earth can't hold its dead. They rise and watch us. They draw us to them.'

'Askew, man.'

'What brought you here to Stoneygate, Kit?'

'My Grandma died, and . . .'

'Death drew you back. Death called you to it. Christopher Watson, aged thirteen. Even your gravestone waited for you, just as it waited for John Askew, aged thirteen.'

He leaned forward, gripped my wrist.

I gripped the ammonite.

'I want you to come with me, Kit. Come with me. Come and properly play the game called Death.'

'Askew. Let me go.'

'I could show you things, Kit. Things that'd give you all the stories you'll ever need.'

His grip tightened. The dog growled. The children whispered in fright. He started to pull me.

'This is why you're like me,' he said. 'Because we know about the darkness of the past, because we know about the darkness of the dead.'

'Yes,' I said. 'But we also know about the light of the present, the light of the living. We could play the game of Life together, Askew. Be my friend. Come back to

Stoneygate. Come back to the living.'

He grunted like a beast. He pulled me tighter. I felt the violence in his grip begin to overcome the yearning in his eyes.

'You!' he hissed. 'Bloody you!'

I struck him with the ammonite at the centre of his brow. I struck again. He reeled backwards, blood already flowing to his face. I started to run, slithering and sliding on the snow. I heard the dog running at my heels. I gripped the ammonite, prepared to strike again, then Askew called:

'Jax! Leave him!'

I leapt the fence, hurried to the gate. I stood there, heard his deep voice following me:

'I'll call you, Kit Watson. You know that, don't you? And when I call, I know you'll come.'

Turned, looked back, saw nothing but moonlight on frozen snow.

I tiptoed back into the house, into my room.

Lak's mother crouched against the wall. She sighed with the relief of my return. She held the stones out, formed the silent words, *Bring him home.*

Twenty Seven

Midwinter's Day, last day at school, end of the winter term. The year's shortest day. The longest night was soon to come.

Allie was bright and thin in green leggings and a bright red coat. She'd gelled her hair and it stuck out in spikes around her grinning face. She danced in the snow at my side.

'Well?' she giggled. 'Well?' She stood with her hands on her hips and grinned and grinned.

'Yes,' I said. 'You were brilliant. Bloody brilliant.'

'Ha! Hahaha! And I terrified you all, didn't I?'

'Yes, Allie.'

'Haha! And you couldn't take your eyes off me. You couldn't take your great goggling eyes off me. Could you, Mr Watson?'

'No, Allie. We couldn't. That's right.'

'And I was best when I was evil, wasn't I? When I turned good again at the end you wanted me to go back and be evil again so you could be terrified again. That's right, isn't it, Mr Watson?'

'Yes, Allie.'

'Hahaha! I was brilliant! And tonight I'll be even brillianter! Won't I, Mr Watson?'

'Yes, Allie. You will.'

'Jeez, Kit! I love it! I just love it!'

I watched her cartwheeling and skipping. I walked on towards school. She gripped my arm.

'I'll do it, you know,' she said. 'I'll really be an actress one day. You'll see me on the telly. You'll say, *That's Allie Keenan. That's my friend.*'

I nodded. 'And I'll write a play for you,' I said.

Her eyes widened. 'Yes!' she said. 'What about?'

'Dunno. Stoneygate.'

'Stoneygate! You're joking!'

'Yes. Stoneygate. I'll call it *The Game Called Death.* It'll start in Askew's den. It'll be winter. He'll be a dark heavy brute and you'll be the a glittering life force and somebody like me'll be in between you both and all confused. You'll work magic and conquer death and bring everybody out into the light. Something like that.'

'Jeez, Kit.' She clapped her hands. 'Then we'll both be famous!' And she cartwheeled again in the snow.

'Askew came back last night,' I said.

'Eh?'

'Last night. After the play. I went out and met him by the river again.'

'Jeez, Kit.'

'Unless I dreamed it. Unless I just imagined it.'

'He's not dead then?' she said.

I shook my head. 'Didn't think he was. Didn't believe all those stupid stories. He's a big daft brute, that's all.' I held her arm. 'Nobody else knows,' I said. 'You haven't to tell anybody.'

'Why should you care what anybody knows about him?'

'There's more to Askew than there seems,' I said.

She shook her head. 'Cave man. Lout. That's all.'

'I think he needs some friends, Allie.'

She just stared at me, then she shrugged.

'Not much chance of that then, eh? Anyway, got other things to think about than him.' She posed again, hands on hips. 'Alison Keenan, actress, life force, aged thirteen.'

We walked on again towards school.

'You'll come to see me again tonight?' she said.

I shrugged.

'You will, Kit? Won't you? When you're there I'm stronger.'

'Yes,' I said.

But I didn't look at her. I already thought that there would be other purposes for me tonight.

Twenty Eight

A useless day. The teachers all distracted, the kids all wild. We pulled Christmas decorations from the walls. We ripped old notes out of files and stuffed them into black bin bags. Girls wrapped tinsel in their hair and linked arms and sang carols and giggled and danced. Out in the yard, the games were crazier than ever: kids slid in great struggling bunches on their backs across the ice, yelled threats and curses at each other, shrieked like demons, pummelled each other with huge handfuls of frozen snow. The sun hung low above them, following its lowest, meanest path of the year. In the hall at the heart of the school the actors rehearsed *The Snow Queen* yet again, preparing to make Midwinter's performance the best of all. I moved through the classrooms and corridors like a ghost. I was silent. I couldn't join in. I could hardly think. I kept wanting to run, to disappear from this place. I knew that something was hunting me, watching me, biding its time before it leapt to capture me and carry me away.

I met Allie at lunch time. She wore the silver on her face

and all she could talk about was the play. She told me how brilliant it would be, how brilliant she would be.

'You'll come again?' she said. 'You will, Kit, won't you?'

I closed my eyes, shrugged. 'Yes,' I muttered.

'You've got to, Kit,' she said. 'I need you to. You don't know how much I depend on you.'

I looked past her, through the plate glass windows that lined the corridor. Beyond the wild kids in the yard I saw Askew's mother at the gates with her baby in her arms. She peered in, seeking her boy.

'You will, Kit, won't you?' said Allie.

She gripped my arm. I pulled away from her.

'Oh, Allie,' I said. 'Why's it always you you want to talk about? Why's it always precious bloody brilliant you?' And I ran from her, back towards the depths of the school.

He was waiting for me in a dark place, a place where two windowless corridors crossed, a place that had been lit by Christmas lights that now lay tangled among pine needles on the floor beneath a naked tree.

'Watson,' he hissed. 'Christopher Watson.'

He stood half-hidden by the tree. Pale hair, pale face, pale voice. Bobby Carr. 'Kit Watson,' he hissed.

I said nothing, just halted, stared at him.

'Yes,' he said. 'You. Kit Watson.'

I heard the screaming from the yard outside, the weird squeaky music from the hall. It came from miles away, years away.

'He wants you.'

'Eh?'

'Eh? Eh? He wants you. He's sent for you.'

I couldn't speak, couldn't think.

'Now,' said Bobby. He stepped out from beside the tree. 'Now,' he said.

He stood beside me, skinny and pale.

'He said you'd come, Kit. He said he knew you'd come.'

I looked back to where I'd come from. I saw a bunch of first years in tinsel and baubles rampaging out into the light.

'This way,' he whispered.

And I followed him, through the corridor, through a back door, past the kitchens, past the waste bins, out into the yard, across a steel pointed fence, out into the wilderness. I stared back at the school, saw Askew's mother, in the yard itself now, moving with her baby through the knots of frantic kids.

'This way,' he said. 'Don't look back.'

He led me out of the wilderness towards Stoneygate's fringes, past ancient pit cottages, past The Fox, Askew's potholed cul-de-sac, out into the hawthorn-hedged lanes, on to the slopes of the hills that stretched upward to dark distant moors and an icy sky. The snow crunched and crackled beneath our feet. Unseen birds screeched as if in panic. We didn't speak apart from Bobby's *This way, this way, don't look back.*

The sun already fell towards the west. Midwinter's Day, the shortest day, the longest night to come.

The hawthorn lanes gave way to open land, ancient tussocky paddocks and fields with ruined dry stone walls around them. Our feet broke the hard surface of the snow. We waded knee-deep, struggled upwards, clothes sodden, icy water seeping into our bones. I turned once more, saw the rooftops of Stoneygate, dark lines of coal smoke rising vertically from them. Heard the children's distant squeals.

'Don't look back,' said Bobby, and we turned away, into a narrow valley. Bare thorn bushes clustered around a thin stream. There were little frozen waterfalls, great gashes in the banks made by playing kids and ancient miners. Stone and soil and the roots of heather and shrubs all entangled. Followed the stream uphill, felt the ice deepening its grip. Looked back, saw nothing, just the frozen slopes we'd followed, the gash of this valley. Came to a flatter area, a broad bank by the stream that faced a steep rocky slope with twisted hawthorn trees before it.

Bobby paused there, watched me. The sun was already behind the valley's edge. We already stood in darkening shadow. The longest night had already begun.

Bobby glanced at his watch, smiled at me.

'S'all right,' he told me. 'This way.'

We walked to the hawthorn, twisted through the dense branches, ripped our clothes and skin on the thorns, came to the head-high hole in the rock, the entrance to the ancient drift mine. The boards that had once covered this place were propped against the rock. KEEP OUT was written on them. A skull and crossbones was printed on them. DANGER OF DEATH.

Bobby grinned again.

'This way, Mr Watson,' he whispered, and he led me into the dark.

Twenty Nine

Pale light filtered from the entrance as we stepped inside. I saw the low arch of bricks over our heads. Then bare rock walls, bare rock roof, a few twisted pitprops and lintels. Other pitprops had given way, and the tunnel was blocked by heaps of rubble where the walls and roof had fallen in.

Bobby's face bloomed as he clambered over the first heap and turned to me. 'This way, Mr Watson.'

There was a narrow gap before him, that would lead us further into the dark. I stood still. What was I doing there? There was nothing to stop me from going out into my life again.

He sniggered.

'It's taken a hundred years for this lot to fall in,' he said. 'Mebbe it'll last another hundred years or more.'

He scrambled through the gap. His feet disappeared, then his face was there, grinning back at me. 'Frightened, Mr Watson?'

'He's really in there?'

'Really. Really, really, really.' He reached his hand out. 'Want a pull, eh?'

I gritted my teeth and scrambled after him, crawled through the gap, slithered through into the deeper dark. He waited for me there, squatting on the rockfall.

'Brave boy, Mr Watson,' he whispered.

Our voices hung in the dead still icy air. There was a smell of coal and dust and damp. My soaked trousers clung to my flesh. I trembled, thought of home, of the warm kitchen. I told myself, "Don't do this. Go home." But I knew that there was no turning back, that I was both driven and drawn into the darkness that lay before us. I reached into my pocket, gripped the ammonite.

'That's the hard bit, Mr Watson. It all gets easy now.'

I said nothing.

'Scared?' he whispered.

I heard the snigger in his voice. 'Just take me to him,' I said.

He moved on. 'Keep low,' he told me. 'Watch the fallen rocks.'

I knocked my head and shoulders against lintels, pit props and rock. I tripped on rubble. I kept my eyes on Bobby before me, his low stooped figure, tried to follow in his tracks. Then we saw it, a frail flickering light from further in.

'Look,' he whispered. 'You see?'

'That's him?'

'That's him.'

I shuddered, moved more quickly through the shadows

towards the light, then stood stockstill. The black snarling dog stood silhouetted against the flames that burned at its back. Then Askew's voice, 'Down, Jax!' Then Askew's own silhouette, his bitter laughter.

'Mr Watson,' he whispered. 'Do come in.' He laughed. 'Didn't I say I'd choose the time and place?'

The tunnel opened out here, before dividing into two. The small fire burned at the centre. Hawthorn branches and pit props were heaped against one wall. There was a bucket of melting snow beside the fire, two skinned rabbits on a metal plate, skewers and forks, a small axe, a sheath knife, a packet of cigarettes. There was a heap of blankets. The dog crouched, watching me, teeth and eyes glittering, saliva drooling from its loose mouth.

'Make yourself at home,' said Askew.

He squatted by the fire. He threw a handful of hawthorn twigs into the flames and in the sudden flare I caught sight of the beasts and demons grinning from the walls, the scratched-in names. He leaned his face close to the flames and lit a cigarette.

'Askew,' I said. 'This is lethal. If there's gas around . . .'

'Kaboom!' he whispered. 'Kaboom! Great flash of fire and light and we're all gone.'

Bobby giggled.

'Worm,' said Askew.

We faced each other across the flames. I saw the congealed blood on his brow. There was a scarf of rabbit skins around his throat. His hair was matted and wild.

'I knew you'd come,' he said. 'There's something in you, not like the rest of the rabble. I knew you'd come.'

'Your mother's searching for you, Askew.'

He lowered his eyes.

'She cries and carries the baby everywhere and searches for you.'

'Thinks I'm dead, eh? Mebbe how it'll all turn out. Mebbe better that way.'

'Come back with me, Askew.'

He threw more wood into the flames. He loosened his shirt. There were animals and faces painted on to his chest. He wore a necklace of coal fragments, wizened hawthorn berries, rabbit bones, a tiny animal skull. He lifted the skinned rabbits with his filthy hands, skewered them, hung them between stones across the fire. He grunted and whimpered.

'Uh. Uh. Ayeeeee.'

Laughed at me.

'Cave man,' he said. 'That's what they used to say, what I used to hear. Bloody cave man. Uh. Uh. Ayeeee. Now they're right.'

Bobby laughed again and Askew leapt at him, pressed him to the earth and knelt over him. He reached out, grabbed the axe, held it high above Bobby's head.

'Ayeeee!' he called. 'Ayeeee! Die, you worm!'

He brought the axe down, then paused, with the blade an inch away from Bobby's face. Glanced at me.

'Mercy. Cave man shows the worm some mercy.'

He glared into Bobby's eyes.

'Now go,' he hissed. 'Tell no one. If you do, I'll find you. Jax will rip you limb from limb.'

'Limb from limb,' repeated Bobby in a tiny trembling voice.

Askew stood up, yanked Bobby to his feet, shoved him on his way. We watched him disappear into the dark, heard his stumbling feet as he hurried out towards the longest night. Then Askew turned to me, and I saw it in his eyes: *You're on your own down here, Mr Watson.*

He put the axe down, threw more twigs on to the flames, stripped his shirt off, crouched half-naked, skin glistening in the firelight, eyes heavy, filled with darkness.

'This is Death,' he whispered.

Thirty

Jax crouched in the entrance, ripped at some bloody bones. Teeth and eyes glittered. Saliva drooled. He kept watching, growling.

I rubbed my eyes. They stung with smoke from the burning hawthorn, from the scorched rabbit's flesh. Smoke hung low over us, it swelled gently into the surrounding tunnels.

Askew watched and smiled. 'We've disappeared, Kit,' he said. 'That's Death. That's truly Death.'

'Askew, man,' I whispered.

He looked at me, then at the wall. I followed his eyes, saw it written there: *John Askew, aged thirteen. Christopher Watson, aged thirteen.*

'Me and you,' he whispered.

'Not me and you. It was long ago. They were poor children forced into the pit. Now dead and gone.'

'Dead and gone?' He smiled. We listened. We heard them, through the crackling of twigs and the hissing of flesh. They whispered in the tunnels. We raised our eyes and saw them there, half-obscured by the smoke, half-hidden by the dark: our poor little children staring at us from the past.

'See?' he whispered.

'Yes, I see.'

'I know you do. There's them that do and them that don't. You and me, we're just the same.'

He turned the rabbits on their skewers. Blood and fat dripped into the flames.

'You didn't pretend,' he said.

'Eh?'

'Eh? Eh? You didn't pretend. When we played the game you didn't pretend.'

'No, I didn't pretend.'

'Everything disappeared. There was nothing.'

'Yes.'

'That's Death. There's them that know what it is to die. There's them that know nothing. You and me, we're just the same.'

He licked his fingers, threw more twigs onto the flames.

'John Askew, aged thirteen,' he whispered. 'Christopher Watson, aged thirteen.'

'Askew, man. Come on out.'

He laughed. He lifted the sheath knife. He pointed it at me.

'We can't. We have come into this place to play the game called Death.'

He watched me.

'I could do anything to you down here.' His eyes glittered

beneath his dark hair, from his blackened face. 'You know that, don't you?' he said.

'Yes.'

'Why did you come, then?'

I shrugged, didn't know what to say. 'Dunno,' I said. 'Something about you. Dunno.'

'About us, Kit. The cave man and the good bright boy. John Askew and Kit Watson. We're just the same.'

He dropped the knife into the dirt.

'It's not a game,' he said. 'I wanted to take you with me. Christopher Watson. I wanted to make you disappear, then disappear myself. Wanted both of us to disappear from the world, to become like the ancient children from the ancient pit.'

He smeared his hands across his chest. The faces there twisted and blurred. He dipped his fingers into the ash at the fire's edge, scraped long black marks across his cheeks.

'Down here,' he said. 'There's no day, no night. You're half-awake and half-asleep, half-dead and half-alive. You're in the earth with bones and ghosts and darkness stretching back a million million years into the past.'

He threw more twigs into the fire. The flames flared, smoke rolled into the tunnels, the demons sneered from the walls.

I rubbed my eyes and Askew grinned.

'That's right,' he hissed. 'Keep your eyes clear. Keep watching, Kit.' He held a cigarette out. 'Take a drag, Kit.'

I took a drag. My head reeled. He laughed. His wild face

and glistening body rocked through the light. His necklace swung. He raised the axe and thumped it into the earth.

'Tell us a story, Kit,' he said.

'Eh?'

'Eh? Eh? Hahaha. I'll tell one, then.'

He thumped the axe into the earth again.

'There was a boy,' he whispered, 'with a drunken father. The father's face was black with rage and red with drink. He raged against his son. He called him stupid lout. He thumped him as a little boy and he thumped him harder as he grew. Sometimes he thumped him until the boy's skin beneath his clothes was black and bruised and his head stung. He whispered to the boy that he'd be better dead, he'd be better if he'd never come into the world. Sometimes he thumped him so that there was nothing left but silence, nothingness, deadness, so that there was no boy left. He'd simply disappeared. Till he started waking up again and it all began again.'

He thumped the axe into the earth.

'Askew,' I whispered.

He threw more twigs onto the flames.

'Keep watching, Kit,' he said. 'Keep listening. You hear the skinny children whispering and whimpering? That's right, Kit.'

I saw the tears running from his eyes.

'I've seen him howling across the wilderness for you,' I said. 'I've seen him weeping for you.'

'It's him I have to kill, Kit. Not you. Me and Jax, we'll get him.'

'Askew, man.'

He threw more twigs on to the flames. He rocked and reeled. He thumped the axe into the earth.

A half-seen little body rushed past us, shimmered in the smoke, flickered in the light.

'Silky!' I whispered.

He passed us again. He paused at the edge of the light, turned his eyes to us, hurried on into the dark.

'Yes, Silky,' said Askew. 'Little Silky. Same as ever. But listen, Kit. Down here, I see the ghosts of deeper darkness. I see them rising from the deepest darkness of the past. I see John Askews and Kit Watsons and little Silkies from a thousand thousand years ago. They come to me because I see them and I bring them back. Ayeeeee! Ayeeeee!'

He thumped his chest. He wiped more ash marks on to his skin. He tilted his head back and roared like a beast.

'Ayeee! Ayeeee!'

He leaned towards the flames and gasped. 'Help me, Kit,' he said.

'Eh?'

'Eh? Eh? Help me bring them back. Help them to appear. Agh! Agh!'

He threw more twigs onto the flames. He sucked on a cigarette. He thumped the axe into the earth. He stared into the tunnels.

'Keep watching, Kit,' he whispered. 'Squeeze your eyes. Squint. Watch them come.'

I watched, saw nothing.

'I've seen them,' he whispered. 'I've really seen them. Agh! Agh!'

I reached out towards him, touched his shoulder.

'Askew, man,' I said. 'Askew.'

'Agh!' he muttered. 'Agh!'

He slumped, pulled his shirt back on, pulled it close about him. Shivered. Hunched beside the fire. I placed hawthorn branches on to the fire. I picked two blankets from the heap, wrapped one around Askew and one around myself. I scooped water from among the melting snow and drank. I turned the rabbits on the skewers. I thought of the deepening night outside. I thought of my mother's eyes as her understanding of my disappearance deepened. I rubbed my eyes, gazed at the frightened children watching from the dark, little Silky brightest of them all.

'I wrote a story for you,' I said. 'I was going to bring it to you. Then you were gone.'

He was silent. He drank frozen snow from his cupped hands. He lit a cigarette. I touched his shoulder again.

'You're right,' I said. 'You and me, we're just the same.'

'Are you my friend?' he whispered.

'Yes, John. I'm your friend.'

Thirty One

The rabbits were scorched black outside and bloody inside. We ate them in silence, slurped and drooled. Saliva and grease and blood trickled from our lips. Jax squatted between us with his bones.

'There's good in everyone,' I said.

He spat into the fire.

'There is,' I said. 'Just a matter of finding it, bringing it out into the light.'

'I've dreamed for years of doing it,' he said. 'Dreamed of how I'd do it. Dreamed of rocks and knives and poison. Dreamed of us standing over him, seeing him dead. Dreamed of how happy we'd be.'

I clicked my tongue. 'That's stupid, man.' I saw the darkness in his eyes as he turned them to me.

'Careful, Kit,' he whispered.

The dog curled his lip and growled.

'It is,' I said. 'It's you they need, not some stupid wild kid with a hatchet in his fist.'

There was long silence. We chewed the rabbits. Then he

turned his eyes to me again. He threw the remains of the rabbit into the fire. He lifted the axe. He drew its blade across his thumb tip. The blood bulbed, then ran free. He held the axe towards me.

'Give me your hand,' he said. 'Let me cut you.'

I watched his eyes, I held out my hand. He gripped it. He sliced the axe blade through my thumb tip. He pressed our wounds together, held our thumbs tight between his fist. We gazed deep into each other eyes.

'Now I feel you entering me. You feel me entering you. John Askew, aged thirteen, Christopher Watson, aged thirteen. Just the same Joined in blood.'

He freed our hands. He lit a cigarette. I nibbled the rabbit bones. The skinny children watched. Silky watched.

'Taste the blood,' he said.

'Eh?'

'Taste the blood on your thumb.'

I licked my thumb, the metallic sour taste of blood.

'Which blood is mine and which is yours?' he asked.

I shook my head.

'No way of knowing, Kit. The taste's the same.'

'That's right,' I said.

'And almost the same as the rabbit's blood you've just tasted.'

'That's right. And almost the same as bear's blood or deer's blood.'

'Ha. Dead right, Kit. The blood of beasts, the blood of people, they're just the same.'

He pulled his blanket closer and stared into the flames.

I rubbed my eyes, shook my head, squinted, saw him as a boy in a bearskin, baby held against his chest.

I gasped.

'What?' he said.

'Nothing. Tired. Falling to sleep.'

'More blankets there,' he said.

I shook my head.

I rubbed my eyes. I scooped melted snow from the bucket. I saw the bearskin again, covering Askew's shoulders. I heard the baby whimpering.

'They need you, Askew. They love you. If you go back you can help them. They'll have someone to protect them. Even your father would have someone to protect him from himself.'

He stared at me, narrowed his eyes as if he stared at a low bright sun. I shuddered. I rubbed my eyes, my ears, shook my head. I chewed my lip. The baby whimpered from its place by Askew's heart.

I caught my breath again. 'Askew!' I gasped.

'What is it?'

I shook my head. 'Nothing. Dreams. Nothing.' I reached across at him, touched his arm. 'Askew. Come back home. Keep the baby safe.'

Narrowed his eyes again. Reached inside the bearskin, whispered words of comfort. The skinny children sighed. They were closer now, edging in from the deepest dark. They watched, watched.

I shook my head, looked at my watch. So late. Deep into the deepest night. My head swam with smoke and sleep and shifting visions. I closed my eyes and saw a night so dark and long it went on forever. Opened them and saw Lak watching from the bearskin.

'What was the story?' said Askew.

'The story?'

'The one you would have brought to me.'

'About a boy, from a long long time ago.'

The baby whimpered. I reached out and touched Askew's arm.

'It's you,' I said.

'Who else?'

'I'm tired, Askew. Need to sleep.'

'There's blankets there.'

He threw more wood on to the fire. The smoke and flames intensified. We wrapped ourselves in blankets and lay down on the stony ground beside the fire. Closed my eyes, saw Lak's mother crouching before me, pebbles held out in her fist, mouth opening and closing: *Bring him home*.

'Tell it to me.'

'I'm tired, John.'

'Tell it to me.'

Bring him home, she said.

The baby whimpered from Askew's heart.

'What was his name?' said Askew.

I looked through the flames, saw his eyes staring from

within the bearskin. I closed my eyes. I gathered the threads of the story.

'His name was Lak,' I murmured, and I set off into the tale as if it were a dream.

Thirty Two

As I began, she came out from the deepest darkness, from the depths of the earth, the depths of time. She came through the longest tunnel into the fringes of the light. She paused a moment there, behind the skinny children, behind Silky, then came on again, came past them, through them. I watched through narrow squinting eyes. I watched her flickering and shifting beyond the flames. I watched her come into this wider space. She was wrapped in animal skins. Skins were tied around her feet. She squatted by the wall, beneath the beasts and names and demons. She rested her eyes upon me. I murmured the story. There was anguish in her eyes as I told of the great struggle in the cave, the loss of her baby, the disappearance of Lak.

'I see it all,' said Askew. He lay there with his eyes closed. 'I'll draw it perfectly.'

'That's great,' I whispered.

'Go on,' he said. 'Don't stop. Go on.'

I told the story to the two of them. I squinted, met her eyes, saw her joy at Lak's victory over the bear, her wretchedness at the return to the empty cave. She seemed about to speak to me, to explain perhaps, to tell me the route that Lak and the baby must take. But she just held up her hands, frustrated, mouthed the words at me: *Bring them home. Bring them home.*

'You've stopped again,' said Askew. 'Keep going. Don't drop off to sleep.' He looked at me, saw nothing but me. 'Go on,' he whispered.

I told the tale. I told of the killing of the deer, of the drinking of the deer's milk and blood, of the hope that grew in Lak's heart. He moved quickly now, heading south. The baby slept against him, contented. Behind them, the great dark birds spiralled from the sky, flapped heavily down into the hollow.

All day they walked the crags above the ice. He trickled melted snow into the baby's mouth. He murmured comfort to her. He nibbled at the strips of deer meat. The short day ended. Night came on. They sheltered in a shallow cave above a rock face. Lak built a fire with the twigs of stunted thorny trees that grew out from the rock. He lay sleeping against the dog Kali with the baby safe and warm between them. He dreamed of his family. He dreamed of being with them in a high-arched cave. There was a bank of grass outside, then a river flowing free beneath the sun that blazed from the centre of the sky. The green valley stretched upward to thickly forested mountains. Fish leapt and glittered. There were trees heavy with fruit. Long grasses arched beneath the burden of their seeds. The family sprawled at ease on the riverbank. The baby lay naked on soft turf with bright flowers growing all around her. She kicked her legs, waved her arms, gurgled with joy. Just a dream. He woke to a new bitter day, the sun inching up into the icy sky, the fire gone out, ice creeping into his bones. They drank melted ice, nibbled deer meat, a handful of harsh berries from the stunted trees, and walked on. Their journey seemed endless to Lak. Endless mountains all around, endless sheets of ice. Short cold days, long dark bitter nights. Nothing to guide them but the low sun that drew them south. They slept in shallow caves, in crevices in the rock. Lak killed another deer one day. Kali brought a rabbit that dangled bloodily from his teeth. Below them in the valleys they saw bear and mammoth and bison. Dark birds gathered above them each day in the sky. The baby in the bearskin grew thinner, thinner. The dog shuffled and whined. Lak's skin crumpled upon his bones. His hands trembled as he touched the baby's lips with water, as he struck the flints to make their fires. Each day he woke and touched her with his trembling hands and each time was certain she'd be dead. They struggled on, towards the sun, until there was no strength left, no hope left, no way to go on. Lak stumbled through the morning, then skidded on a patch of ice, slipped, tumbled down into a gully, lay there unconscious on the ice. He woke again, but only to give himself and his baby sister up for dead. He reached inside the bearskin, felt her cold and still against him. He breathed a final prayer to the Sun God, that they would be taken quickly, before the birds came down. Then held his sister close, and beneath the shallow noonday sun slipped quickly with her down into the deepest dark.

I paused. I squinted through the flames. She held her hands against her face. Tears ran through her fingers. She watched me, begged me.

'Don't stop,' whispered Askew.

He lay with his face turned towards the fire, eyes closed, as if he were sleeping. In the flickering light his blanket turned to bearskin and then to wool again. In the hissing of the fire the baby's whimpers could be heard. The world slipped moment by moment into a distant past and back again.

'Go on, Kit. Just go on.'

'Askew,' I whispered.

'What is it?' He looked at me. I turned my eyes towards Lak's mother.

'There,' I whispered.

He looked through the dying flames.

'Narrow your eyes, John. Squint.'

'What is it?'

Then he caught his breath, and stared.

'Yes,' he said. 'I told you, didn't I?'

He held up his palm to her, as if to greet her. She watched us both with yearning eyes.

'Go on,' he whispered. 'Don't stop, Kit. Keep going on.'

I closed my eyes, gathered again the threads of the tale, set off again.

He held the baby tight. She was still and silent. He descended through the dark with her. He heard the voices of his ancestors – the voices of the dead, calling him, welcoming him. He felt their fingers touching him, guiding him towards them. He entered the great cave into which all the dead descend, the cave where no fire burns, where no sun lights the entrance. And rested there, crouched against the wall, the baby by his heart, the unseen ancestors all around. It was her whimpering that brought the light, a tiny chink of it. She whimpered again, frail, high-pitched. She shifted in her wrappings. Her tiny fingers scrabbled against his chest. She cried out more loudly. He shifted, opened his eyes, the light intensified. He found her trapped beneath him. He rolled so that she lay within the bearskin at his side. The light was brilliant and endless, glaring down into the narrow gully, so bright he couldn't turn his eyes towards its source. The baby wailed and screamed, filling the world with her voice, her hunger, her refusal to die, her demand for life. He tried again to turn his eyes towards the sun, but couldn't bear it. There was sweat drenching his skin, fire burning in his bones. He looked downwards from the gulley, down across the crags into the valley, down to a sparkling free river, fruit trees, long grasses. A herd of deer moved slowly across the slopes. Flights of brightly-coloured birds flew below the crags. And there were people there, lightly-clad, with necklaces, paintings on their bodies, feathers in their hair. Lak stared. The baby screamed, and within the screams Lak heard the words: *These things will come again. These things will come again. These things will come again.*

The ice returned. The frozen valley. The low sun. The

hunger in his belly. He held the baby close, he trickled melted ice into her mouth. He clambered from the gulley, set off across the crags. He had known the sun at the centre of the sky. The words of the Sun God had entered his heart. That day he began to see people in furs on the ice below him, and he descended with his courage towards them.

Thirty Three

As Askew listened, I saw his head drop. His breathing deepened and lengthened. Jax slept as well. The embers faded. Lak's mother watched with gentle eyes. I pulled my blankets close, entered again the ever-running tale. I murmured of Lak's days on the ice, of the shelter he gained with families not his own. I told of baby's growing strength. I described the patches of green that began to appear within the ice as they moved south, the channels of freely-flowing water, the sun that climbed a little higher in the sky. He heard rumours of his family. There were tales of sightings and encounters. Yes, he was told. This family carried the tale of the theft of a baby by a bear, of the loss of a son in its pursuit. Lak followed the tales and rumours. Many days of walking, listening, until he was pointed towards a riverbank where grass had started growing through the ice, where tiny bright blooms shone among the grass, where the entrance to a cave was. Lak hesitated at the entrance. Deep inside, a fire burned. Figures hunched about it.

The baby whimpered, the dog whined.

'Ayee!' called Lak softly. 'Ayee!' His voice echoed faintly from the rock within.

'This is Lak!' he called. 'This is the baby Dal carried next to Lak's heart. Ayee! Ayee!'

Askew stirred in his sleep. He grunted. Lak's mother sat with her arms outstretched, prepared to welcome her baby and her son. I gazed into her eyes.

Lak stepped inside. 'This is Lak,' he called. 'This is the baby Dal.'

The faces above the fire turned towards him. The children, and the father, who was so frail, so shrunken now. His mother gasped with joy, spread her arms to welcome her baby and her son.

We gazed at each other across the fading embers.

Askew stirred again in his sleep, then settled.

'Go on,' I whispered. 'Go on.'

He rose from his place by the fire. He opened the bearskin. He showed the baby held safe against his heart. His mother stood and took him in her arms.

I watched. I waited for the vision to fade now that the tale was told. Then the mother released her son and came to me. She stooped down to me. I saw the tears in her eyes and felt her breath on me. She took my hand and pressed the brightly-coloured pebbles into it. She touched my cheek. Then went with her son out of the ring of light cast by the embers, past the ring of staring faces, back into the deepest dark

I slept. Just blackness all around. Knew nothing more, until

Silky came running and flickering into me, and Grandpa held me tight.

'Kit,' he whispered. 'Kit.'

'Grandpa!'

'Don't worry, Kit. They'll come for us.'

Thirty Four

I lay a million years there, by the dead fire in the dead dark with my Grandpa holding me. Then the distant footsteps came. The flickering of a lamp.

'John,' I whispered. I reached across the cold ashes, touched him. 'John.'

He grunted, stirred. 'What?'

Somewhere in the darkness, Jax growled.

'Down, boy,' said Askew.

The footsteps came nearer. A torchbeam flickered on the walls.

'Will you come out now?' I whispered.

No answer.

'John,' I said.

'Yes, I'll come.'

'Kit! Kit Watson!'

I smiled. Allie's voice, echoing through the tunnel to us.

'Here!' I called. 'We're here!'

'Kit! Kit!'

'Allie!'

'I dreamed all night about the baby,' said Askew. 'About holding her, keeping her safe. Like the boy in the story with his sister.'

We heard Allie coming closer, calling.

'There was a space against my heart where she once was and I needed her there to fill it again.' He reached out and gripped my wrist. 'It happened, didn't it? We saw those things.'

'Yes,' I said.

'And it was me that went with her? A part of me?'

'Yes. I watched you go to her then disappear with her.' I felt the pressure of pebbles in my palm. I kept my fist clenched tight.

'When I woke,' he said, 'I wasn't sure where I was. I thought I'd wake with her and the baby, in a cave a thousand thousand years in the past.'

I heard the catch in his breath. He sniffed.

'I'm scared,' he whispered.

'It's OK, John. I'll try to help. We're joined in blood.'

Then Allie came. She swept the torchbeam across us. We sat up, wrapped in filthy blankets by the cold fire. Jax growled softly, wagged his tail as the light crossed him. We couldn't see her properly, just a black figure behind the source of the light.

'Jeez, Kit!' she said. 'Jeez, Kit!'

She came and crouched beside us. She shone the torch across herself. She had her ice girl clothes on, her skin was silver and her nails were claws.

'There's all hell on,' she said. 'They're dragging the river for you. Your parents came last night and then again this morning. They said I must know something. I said nothing. I didn't tell what you said about Askew. Then I knew it. I went to Bobby Carr and got the worm to spill the beans. But didn't tell them. Didn't want to raise their hopes.'

She shone the torch straight into Askew's black-patterned face.

'Jeez, Askew,' she said. 'Look at you.'

She touched my hand.

'They're desperate, Kit. What's he done to you?'

'Nothing, Allie.'

'You're all right?' she said.

'Yes, we're both all right.'

'Ha. Knew you would be. Knew it'd just be this stupid lout and his stupid games again.' She shone the torch on him again. 'Askew, man. You drive me bloody wild.'

Then she laughed. 'Come on. Get your things and let's get out before the place collapses.'

By the light of the torch, Askew emptied the bucket across the ashes, threw his knife and axe in. We lifted the blankets. I kept my fist clenched tight. We looked one last time into the inner tunnels, saw the watching eyes there, saw Silky's glistening.

'Come on,' she said again. 'What you looking at?' And she led us out.

We stumbled through the tunnel, scrambled through the rock fall, came through the brickwork arch and through the hawthorn. The sun glared down into the narrow valley. We held our arms across our eyes. Allie roared with laughter.

'Look at you! Just look at you!'

And Askew and I looked at each other, the filth and blood on us, our goggling eyes, and even Askew laughed.

I opened my hand, showed the brightly-coloured pebbles there.

'What's those?' asked Allie.

'Gifts,' I said.

Askew reached out and touched the stones. His eyes were shining as he stared into my eyes.

'Jeez,' said Allie. 'What's going on between you two?'

I closed my fist again.

'Don't worry,' I said. 'We'll tell you everything.'

Then we headed down through the deep frozen snow.

Before we turned on to the final slope that would take us into Stoneygate, Allie made us stop. She posed in her silvery clothes, raised her silvery claws, tilted her silvery face towards the sun.

'I put these on for the publicity,' she said. 'There'll be cameras coming to catch the rescuer. The girl who brings back disappeared boys in a story, and brings them back them in real life. Allie Keenan, actress, life force, rescuer, aged thirteen.'

'You look great,' I said.

'Thank you, Mr Watson. Mr Askew?'

'You look great,' he muttered.

Allie nodded. 'We'll have some work to do on your

attitude, Mr Askew. But in the meantime, that will be fine.'

And we walked on towards Stoneygate, the blackened boy with bone necklaces and paintings on him, the good-bad ice girl with silver skin and claws, the wild dog Jax behind, and me between with ancient pebbles in my palm.

Part Three

SPRING

One

The pebbles are on my desk. They're in a dish beside the ammonite, the carved pony, the fossil tree. Grandpa's pitman's lamp is there as well. His wedding photograph is on my wall. His voice is singing in my head, his stories are running through me. Outside, the ice has gone and the wilderness is green. Kids play out there in jeans and T-shirts. They run through the year's first heat haze, they stamp up clouds of dust that hang in the brilliant light. The river's flowing free. Ice never did meet at the centre.

When does Spring begin? In March? On the day the clocks go forward? Or does it really start at dawn on the morning that ends Midwinter's Night? From that moment, the days begin to grow, the nights diminish. The world begins to turn us towards the sun again.

So it was Spring already as we walked back down to Stoneygate from the drift mine. It was Spring when Christmas came. And it was Spring when Grandpa came to stay with us for the final time.

We saw the little police boat on the river. We saw policemen and our neighbours digging in the snow beneath the hawthorn hedges. We saw the huddles of worried adults, the struggling knots of excited kids. We saw the faces turning to us, we heard the exclamations of relief. There they are! Look! There they are! And they came running uphill through the snow to us, astonished to see the disappeared ones brought back into the world as if by magic. They clustered around us, goggled at us as if we were ghosts, as if we were creatures in some weird dream.

'Look at them,' they whispered. 'Look at the state of them.'

The police stood with hands on hips, faces blank, watching, silent. Little kids reached out, touched us, giggled, dashed back to Stoneygate with the news. As we entered Stoneygate, we saw Askew's mother with the baby in her arms coming from the potholed cul-de-sac. She hurried to her son and stood before him and he took her and his sister in his great filthy arms and they cried and cried. She broke away and came to me, with dirt and ash from her son's face smeared on her cheeks, and she gripped my hands. I felt her rings and fingernails pressing into my skin.

'You brought him home,' she said. 'You really brought him home.'

'And me!' said Allie.

'Yes,' said Mrs Askew, and she kissed Allie's silver cheek. 'You as well. Both of you.'

Allie and I walked on. She skipped and danced. She tilted

her silvery face and raised her silvery claws. Yes, she told them. Yes, she was the one who'd known where to look for us, she was the one who'd brought us out. She gripped my arm. 'They were frantic,' she said. 'Desperate with fear.' I trembled as we came to the wilderness, as we entered the lane that led me home, as my parents rushed out of the house at me.

They'd believed I was dead. They'd imagined I'd never be seen again. They'd imagined I'd be brought out on a hook from the river, found frozen in a snow drift, discovered in a dark lane with my skull smashed in or with a knife in my heart. How could I tell them about the power of ghosts and stories, about the caves and tunnels in our heads, about a boy and his mother from the deep dark frozen past? How could I tell them about the dead ones that surround us, about John Askew, aged thirteen, and Christopher Watson, aged thirteen? How could I tell them the truth about the pebbles I carried in my palm? But I told them about Askew's pain and fright, about his loneliness. I told them about the baby inside him that had never had a chance to grow. I told them there was something in him and something in me that kept drawing us together.

'John Askew,' they said. 'That lout, John Askew.'

They inspected me for scars, for damage.

'What did he do to you?' they said.

'Nothing,' I said. 'Nothing. He became my friend.'

There were the same questions from the police. They sat at the kitchen table in their dark uniforms, sipping tea. A woman and a man.

'What did he do to you?' he asked.

'Nothing.'

'You can tell us,' the woman said softly. She touched my arm. 'Don't worry. It's him that'll be in trouble, not you.'

'Really,' I said. 'There was nothing. I went to find him. We talked and we ate rabbits. It got late. We spent the night in the drift mine. Then we came out again.'

The man raised his eyes, shook his head at my parents.

'We could get a doctor to examine him,' he said.

They looked at me.

'No point,' I said. 'There's nothing to find.'

Then I showed the little scar on my thumb.

'Just this,' I said. 'He did it with an axe. We became blood brothers.'

The policeman shook his head again.

'Kids,' he said.

He scribbled in his note book.

'Have you any idea the trouble you've caused?' he said. 'It's not a bloody game, you know.'

They went away. They stood at the front door with my parents. Nothing they could do, I heard. They'd keep an eye on things. They'd talked to the Askew boy but he'd given them nothing to go on. The Askews. The bloody Askews. They knew that family from a long way back. They'd keep an eye on them.

Mum and Dad came back. We sat together and they watched me for a long time, as if by staring and staring they could keep me close to them, as if I'd never again be lost to them. We cried together and we held each other and we said no, nothing like this must happen again. Then we talked about Grandpa coming, and we started to prepare for him.

We cleaned the room next to mine. We made his bed and folded back the covers. We cleaned his wedding photograph and polished his pitman's lamp. We hung baubles and tinsel at his window. We found a special Christmas card: an ancient scene, children playing on a frozen river. We wrote, *Welcome home*, and signed our names with love.

Two

We were in the papers. A reporter came to talk to me but Dad wouldn't let him in. He sent a photographer packing, too. Allie sent a photograph of herself in her costume anyway. She wrote that she was the rescuer, and there was a great story of danger, courage and magic to be told. When the paper came on the Monday, there were just a few lines about Askew and me, and nothing at all about Allie. **BOYS SAFE AFTER NIGHT IN ABANDONED DRIFT MINE**. Underneath it said, **How Long Until These Death Traps Are Sealed Forever?** There was a photograph of the newly bricked-up entrance. There was a long article about the dangers of the old pits, and an announcement of a new campaign to make sure they would all be properly filled in and sealed.

'Typical,' said Allie. 'They wouldn't know a decent story if it slapped them in the face.'

They printed her photo on Christmas Eve on the Local Events page: **Miss Alison Keegan, aged thirteen. A Little Miss Who's Been A Big Hit In St. Thomas' Christmas Play**.

She came running to the door waving the paper in her fist.

'Have you seen it?' she said. She rushed in and spread it on the kitchen table. 'They can't even get my bloody name right! Makes you want to tear your bloody hair out! Nothing about the proper story or even about the bloody part I played! Little Miss! Who do they think I am? Shirley Bloody Temple! Jeez, Kit!'

'Alison!'

It was Mum, standing in the doorway. Allie gasped and bit her lip.

'Sorry, Mrs Watson,' she said.

Mum nodded. 'Glad to hear it.'

'Have you seen it, though?' said Allie. 'Can't even get my . . .'

'I know who that is!' shouted Grandpa from the living room.

Allie looked through, saw him sitting there with a blanket on his knee.

'Mr Watson!' she said.

'Aye,' he said. 'That's the one. And you're that little bad lass, aren't you?'

'Yes! Yes, I am!'

'Well get in here and have a cup of tea with me and stop driving that lad and his mother round the twist!'

Three

Grandpa had come that morning, Christmas Eve. Dad brought him in the car. He tottered into the garden, in his old best suit with a blanket around his shoulders. He stood leaning on his walking stick. His body trembled gently. His eyes were watery. His breath rose in plumes around him. He turned to stare back through the gate.

I went to his side and took his elbow.

'Aye, Kit,' he said. 'It's good to be back home again.'

He leaned on me for a moment, and we gazed together across the wilderness towards the river, where the sun shimmered on ice and water and the air trembled and skinny children played.

I felt his sigh.

'It's a magic place, this world,' Grandpa whispered. 'Always remember that.'

I smiled and helped him in. He was frail and small. His jacket hung loosely from his shoulders. He sat in front of the Christmas programmes on television and sipped tea and nibbled Christmas cake. A carol service came on and he sang along in his trembling voice.

In the deep Midwinter, frosty wind made moan,
Earth stood hard as iron, water like a stone
Snow had fallen, snow on snow, snow on snow
In the deep Midwinter, long ago . . .

Mum and I sat with him. Each time he looked at us it was as if he had to remember us again. Then his eyes would clear and he would smile with joy. He had a glass of sherry and he fell asleep, with his head resting on the wing of the chair and his eyes shifting beneath their lids.

Mum reached out and stroked his hair.

'Lovely man,' she whispered.

She stroked my hair, just the same.

'Stay with him, Kit.'

She turned the television down, and left the room, went on preparing for Christmas Day.

I sat with a notepad, scribbling down the final part of Lak's story, the part I'd told to Askew in the drift mine. As I wrote the final sentences, Grandpa woke and watched me.

'OK?' I whispered.

He narrowed his eyes, squinted, trying to see me clear, trying to remember me.

'It's Kit,' I said.

'That's right. Course it is.' We laughed gently together.

'Off with the fairies, eh?' I said.

He closed his eyes and smiled. 'Head full of caves

and tunnels, son. Keep getting lost in them.'

I scribbled on. He kept staring at me. He sang softly. *When I was young and in me pri-ime . . .*

'I know what it was,' he said.

'Eh?'

'Eh? Eh? It was you, wasn't it? It was me and Silky and you. A few nights back. That's right, isn't it?'

'Yes, Grandpa, that's right.'

He sang again.

'Strange what you remember,' he said. 'Never know these days what's dreams and what's real.'

He nibbled at the Christmas cake, closed his eyes again, fell asleep again.

Then Allie came with the newspaper and he called through to us,

'I know who that is!'

She had tea and Christmas cake with him. He grinned and told her, 'You're the one that drove me missus round the bend and up the pole!'

'That's right!' she giggled. 'That's right, Mr Watson.'

'Bad lass,' he said. 'Good bad lovely lass. Give us a song, then, hinny.'

She stood in front of him. She danced as she sang and reached down and held his hands and swung them as if he was dancing too. They sang together:

Whist, lads, had yer gobs
An I'll tell yez all an aaful story,

Wisht, lads, had yer gobs
An I'll tell ye aboot the worm . . .

Allie sang more softly as the song went on, knelt down and rested his hands in his lap, guiding him as he closed his smiling eyes and drifted back to sleep.

Four

Christmas Day. I woke to his knocking at my door, his little voice. Very early, dawn just breaking. I called him in. He stood there smiling in his dressing gown.

'Happy Christmas, Kit,' he said.

'Happy Christmas, Grandpa.'

He pressed a finger to his lips.

'Come and see,' he whispered.

'Eh?'

'Something for you. Come and see. Tiptoes, mind.'

We slipped into his room. He switched the light on. The tinsel and baubles glittered at the window. He gave me a sheet of white paper with silvery red writing:

To Kit
Happy Christmas
With Love
Grandpa

'This is for you,' he said.

I looked around for a present, saw his souvenirs on the shelves, fossils and little carvings, ancient photographs of his pit mates, the wardrobe with the cuff of a white shirt caught in the door, slippers on the floor, the wedding photograph, his bed with the impression of his frail body on it.

'What is?' I said.

He grinned. 'Everything is. Everything is yours.'

I didn't know what to say.

'Have to hang on to a few of the things a while longer,' he said. 'But afterwards they come to you, to keep or chuck as you wish. Everything.'

I gazed around the room again as the light grew and shone in upon these gifts. His eyes were shining.

'What I'd like to give you most of all is what's inside. The tales and memories and dreams that keep the world alive.' He squeezed my arm.

I touched the photographs, the fossil tree, the shirt cuff, felt how they burned with Grandpa's life, and with those tales and memories and dreams.

'OK?' he whispered.

'Yes.' I put my arms around him, held him as we'd held each other in the darkest tunnels of our dreams. 'Thank you, Grandpa.'

He sighed.

'One day,' he whispered. 'I won't be here any more. You know that, Kit. But I'll live on inside you and then inside your own children and grandchildren. We'll go on forever, you and me and all the ones that's gone and all the ones that's still to come.'

And the light intensified around us, bringing Grandpa's final Christmas Day.

The morning was presents from under the tree, mince pies, sausage rolls and sherry, Dad getting tipsy, parading in his new checked shirt and stinking of aftershave, Mum showing off dangly silver earrings, carols blasting from the CD, the house warm and filled with steam and the smells of turkey and sausage stuffing and spicy pudding. Allie came in red and green with snowflakes melting in her hair and with little gifts for all of us. She sang *Good King Wenceslas* with Grandpa and ate chocolate coins from the tree, and talked too fast and giggled and said she loved Christmas, just loved it. When she left, I stood with her beside the fence. We watched the kids with their new bikes and skates, with Walkmans plugged into their ears. We watched them slithering and sliding and giggling with the joy of it all.

'It's beautiful, isn't it?' she said. 'The place we live.'

'I thought you just wanted to get out of it.'

'I will. But wherever I go, I'll take it with me.'

She kissed me on the cheek and blushed.

'I'm glad you came to Stoneygate, Mr Watson,' she whispered, and she slipped way.

It was almost lunch time when John Askew came.

I was setting the table – knives, forks, wine glasses, table mats – when he knocked at the door.

'I'll get it,' called Mum.

There was silence when she opened it.

I looked through and saw him standing there, thickset, dark-haired, dark-eyed. I hurried to the door and slipped past Mum on to the step.

'John,' I said.

And I laughed, because he opened his coat and showed his baby sister in a sling at his chest. She wore a furry hood, and she grinned out at us.

I saw the suspicion in Mum's eyes, the sudden anger, but saw how it softened as she saw the baby.

'I just brought this,' said Askew.

He held out an envelope. I took the card out. He'd drawn the wilderness with a huge Christmas tree at the centre, with angels hovering around its tip and children playing at its foot. Inside, he'd written simply: *Happy Christmas. John Askew.*

'Your sister's lovely,' said Mum.

He grinned. There was new brightness in his eyes.

'Aye,' he said. 'She's grand.'

I looked at Mum.

'Come on in,' I said.

John shook his head. 'Got to get back,' he said. 'Just came with the card.'

'Yes, come on,' said Mum. 'She'll catch her death out here.'

He came in shyly, awkwardly. He stood in the living room, clumsily shifting his feet. Dad came in and watched him there.

'John brought this,' I said to Dad, and showed him the card.

Askew looked at the tree, at the television, at Grandpa sleeping.

Then he met Mum's eye.

'Sorry about the bother, Mrs Watson, Mr Watson,' he said. 'Won't happen again.'

'Good,' said Mum.

'Kids' games,' said Dad. 'Kids' games, eh? They're over now.' He reached out and took Askew's hand. 'Happy Christmas, John,' he said. 'And to your family.'

'Aye,' said Askew. 'Thank you. Happy Christmas.' He drew his coat across the baby as if to leave.

'John Askew,' said Grandpa, opening his eyes.

'That's right,' I said.

Grandpa stared at him.

'Aye,' he said. 'That's right. Knew your grandfather, son. A good brave man.'

The baby whimpered. Askew opened his coat again and she giggled out at us and Grandpa gasped with delight.

'Peepo,' said Grandpa. 'Peepo, little hinny.'

He grinned. 'Give us a hold, eh?'

'Yes,' said Mum. 'Go on, John.'

Askew lifted the baby from her sling and put her down on Grandpa's lap. Grandpa held her, made a face for her, giggled with her.

'What's her name?' he said.

'Lucy.'

'Peepo, little Lucy. Peepo, bonny lass.'

Then he was silent, and we stood together and watched as the old man and the baby gazed with joy into each other's eyes.

Mum touched John's arm.

'How's Mum?' she asked.

'OK. She's going to be OK.'

'Look after her now, son.'

He nodded. 'Yes, I will.'

The baby giggled.

'Better take her home,' said Askew.

He leaned down to take her.

Grandpa kissed her cheek.

'Bye bye, little Lucy,' he whispered.

Askew closed his coat and I took him out.

'See you, Kit,' he said.

'See you, John. Happy Christmas.'

Back inside the house, we went on preparing for the meal. I lit the candles on the table. Grandpa drifted in and out of sleep. Mum watched me.

'So,' she said. 'What do we make of that, then?'

I shrugged.

'He's all right, you know,' I said. 'He really is all right.'

Then Dad brought the massive steaming turkey in.

'Come on!' he said. 'Action stations! Happy Christmas, everyone!'

Grandpa woke with a start.

'Bye bye,' he said. 'Bye bye lovely Lucy.'

Five

Grandpa died in mid-January. The thaw was starting. Pools of water on the wilderness, snow turning to slush in the lanes, snowdrops peeking through in the gardens and beneath the hawthorn hedges. I was in school. Dobbs was on about the movements of the earth again. He said that if we could move forward a million years, everything we saw before us would have changed: no Stoneygate, no flowing river, no wilderness, no us.

'The earth endlessly reforms itself,' he said. 'The continents shift, the surface cracks, fire bursts out from below. The hills are simply blown away. The sea swells and shrinks. The world tilts on its axis and brings us fiery heat or icy cold. Deserts or the ice cap creep across us. All we see and all we know is engulfed, swallowed up, regurgitated.'

He smiled.

'We are puny little things,' he said. 'The beast called Time is our great predator, and there is no escape from it.' He smiled again. 'However. That is not to say there is no need to do our homework.'

And he dished out sets of worksheets.

It was a little first year who came to the door.

'Please, sir,' she said shyly. 'Christopher Watson is to go to the office, please.'

Mum was waiting there, and she didn't need to say a word.

He was buried beside Grandma in St. Thomas' churchyard. The place where the grave lies can be seen in my grandparents' wedding photograph. The monument with my name on it is nearby. Many people came to his funeral: his remaining pitmates, the descendants of the old families. Allie stood beside me in red and green. John Askew stood further back with his mother and father. There were many tears, but afterwards the house rang with laughter as the reminiscences and stories started.

That night I lay in the dark and listened to the silence through the wall.

'Good night, Grandpa,' I whispered.

I felt his hand in mine.

'Good night, son. Good night.'

Six

John Askew comes to school again now. They allow him two afternoons a week, when there are Art lessons. They've said he can be full-time again, if he can keep the lout in himself under control. He has done the drawings for Lak's story, and they hang in the corridor with my words. They are beautifully-detailed things: the family in the cave, the bear, the world of ice, Lak with the baby in the bearskin, Lak's mother in her animal skins with her arms outstretched to welcome him. Burning Bush says how right I was to choose him as the artist.

'They're wonderful,' she says. 'It's as if he really sees the things he draws. They match your words so beautifully. They're like the heart and soul of the same story.'

'Yes,' I answer. 'Like they're joined in blood.'

'Yes,' she says.

Askew's father has stopped drinking. We no longer see him reeling in the lane. He is stooped and shrunken but Askew's been told that if he looks after himself he'll become a new man. The house in the potholed cul-de-sac is orderly.

The curtains are open at the window, the garden is clean. The baby toddles, holding her mother's hand. She sits giggling on a blanket with her brother. Beyond her are the pit-riddled hills, reaching up towards the distant moors. Up there, they have cleaned out our drift mine. New pit props keep it safe. The tunnel floors are cleared of rubble. There are electric lights. There is a metal gate at the entrance. There are maps pinned there, and explanations of our history. Dobbs has begun to take classes up there. They put on helmets and giggle and bite their lips in fright. An old pitman opens the gate, leads them in, explains the wonders and dangers of the past. Sometimes he switches off the lights and the mine is filled with screaming.

I have brought Grandpa's souvenirs into my room. I sit at my desk and hold them and feel the stories that wait inside them to be told. Often my friends come, and we walk out together into the wilderness, Allie, Askew and me. The wild dog Jax paces behind. Sometimes we hear children whispering that we are the ones who were thought to be dead. The wilderness around us is filled with children playing, with neighbours walking. When we narrow our eyes and squint we see that it is filled with those who have walked and played before. On the brightest days, when the sun pours down and dances on the river and the air begins to tremble, I see Grandpa and Grandma before me. I follow them. I walk beside the river with my friends. I know that as long as there are others to see us, we will walk here together forever.

Look out for *Heaven Eyes*, David Almond's next book publishing in January 2000:

"We come into the world out of the dark. We haven't got a clue where we've come from. We've got no idea where we're going. But while we're here in the world, if we're brave enough, we'll flap our wings and fly."

It's easy. Running away from Whitegates. Erin and her running-away friend January do it all the time. But this time they're going down river. This time they might never come back. This time they're looking for a tiny corner of Paradise.

How could they ever have imagined that what they'd find there would be Heaven Eyes? Heaven Eyes. This girl who should have drowned at sea, this girl rescued from the mud. This girl with a secret history only Grampa knows. And he isn't telling . . .

'The new year starts with what could well be the biggest book of the next twelve months. *Heaven Eyes* is an absorbing read . . . an incredible story. It deals with a myriad of complex and searching issues in Almond's now unmistakable and inimitable style. Both original and unnerving, this really is a fantastic book.'

Nic Knight, Ottakar's, *The Bookseller*